PART 1 of
ROGER ELWOOD'S
Riveting Six-part Adventure

There is a glorious light on the horizon, but first you must experience the terror-filled hours of darkness. . .when no one can be trusted. . .when commonplace occurrences are not what they seem. . .when the future of civilization hinges on one word. . .epidemic.

The serpent has returned. . .not to a garden, but to a world overrun by desperation.

The adventure continues in Parts 2-6, to be released every month through August, 1997.

Roger Elwood, whose gripping suspense titles have occupied best-seller lists over the past ten years, is well known to readers of Christian fiction. Such Elwood page-turners as *Angelwalk, Fallen Angel, Stedfast,* and *Darien* have together sold more than 400,000 copies.

A RIVETING SIX-PART ADVENTURE

PART 1
WITHOUT THE DAWN

HOW SOON THE SERPENT

ROGER
ELWOOD

A Barbour Book

© MCMXCVII by Roger Elwood

ISBN 1-57748-038-4

Published by Barbour & Company, Inc.
        P.O. Box 719
        Uhrichsville, Ohio 44683
        http://www.barbourbooks.com

Member of the
Evangelical Christian
Publishers Association

Printed in the United States of America.

CHAPTER 1

*For those criminals from barrio punks to Mafiosi, the grow-
ing availability of the Internet offered an appeal that they
could not resist because it was a protected means of communication. No ordinary wiretaps were effective or legal, making the World Wide Web momentarily impregnable in that
respect, an environment of unfettered freedom mandated not
only by government edict but also the nature of the Internet
itself, millions of people transmitting from scores of countries
at different times of the day and night.*

*Since regular telephone lines were the standard medium
of communication, law enforcement agencies concentrated
on developing a way of tapping Internet calls as they had
been doing with ordinary phone calls for decades. EWITT, as
it was called, or Electronic Web Intervention Translation Technology, seemed promising since it was able to decipher the
electronic impulses going from one computer to another and
uncover whatever messages were involved—but there were
glitches that would keep it from widespread use for many
months, if not years. Nevertheless, the very possibility of
EWITT or something like it being available sooner or later
raised hopes that there could be at least one effective weapon
against computer-oriented terrorism waged by professional
criminals and street gangs alike, the latter wearing their na-
tionality as a symbol of pride but degrading it with their
actions, causing an underlying suspicion directed against
anyone who was Black or Hispanic. Ku Klux Klan and Aryan
Underground members had another excuse to increase their
attacks, along with a coincident rise in anti-Semitism in an
atmosphere that caused bigotry in many stripes to flourish.*

*However, what no district attorney or chief of police or
attorney general could have known, since none was a modern*

form of an Old Testament prophet, was that they were not looking, as it would turn out, in the direction of those culprits who actually would unleash something far worse than "ordinary" criminals. For example, the Mafia had a certain code of honor that had been guiding it for more than 200 years, and one part of this code was patriotism of a sort, patriotism that was expressed during World War II, when Mafia kingpins across the nation turned their men loose on a single task: find and eliminate Nazi saboteurs as well as other types of spies who had infiltrated the United States from the Third Reich.

The real instigators of what was to become the worst calamity in recorded history knew no such loyalty to country.

And they were everywhere.

During the summer of 1997, in a place two sisters had come to call Eden. . .

Imagining her toes just touching the clear, chilly water of the now familiar greenish-blue lake, Clarice Fothergill stood on the balcony of a chalet not far from L'Abri, Switzerland. L'Abri, the site of a highly regarded retreat— reserved for only the wealthiest of European families—was a short distance from the main hub of Geneva where so much of the history of the entire continent of Europe had been negotiated over the course of the twentieth century. For perhaps the thousandth time, she could see herself at the edge of the lake that spread out for about a quarter of a mile in front of her, certainly not a large body of water when compared to a score of others that could be found throughout Switzerland. Confined on three sides by dwarfing snow-shrouded Alpine mountains, the sapphirelike pool was the dominant feature of a secluded and exquisitely pristine valley, as well as the center of such activities as boating, fishing, swimming, and water skiing.

Clarice sighed as she glanced at her beautiful surroundings: lawns blessed with shiny grass so thick-bladed that it seemed leaflike, a meadowland of flowers sporting as many as fifty different hues, all springing from the darkest, healthiest soil to be found anywhere on the continent. And in the center of this wonderland rested that remarkable, beguilingly pure lake, its surface untroubled except by birds occasionally diving in to catch a beakful of the naturally abundant supply of fish. The elements of that valley came together with what could be called providential precision, forming such a glorious natural tapestry that first-time observers were driven to speculation about whether Eden itself could possibly have been lovelier.

Clarice breathed in deeply of the invigorating air, its coolness refreshing to her lungs, the quietude calming to her nerves. The recent demands of her home life on a medieval estate in the bountiful Yorkshire region of northern England, a life that now seemed to include a slowly dying mother, had caused her untold anxiety.

You have never been here, Mother, because you wanted this to be our special hideaway, where Sarah and I could go not only on vacation but any other time of year if we needed time away, she thought. *Yet I wonder if this blessed air and that pure water could somehow prove healing to you, given the increasingly polluted air of England.*

Since Elizabeth Fothergill had been taken ill more than a year before, and could do not much more than sit back in a chair and gaze out over rolling fields, or be fed by someone else who had the patience to do so, it was up to Clarice to run everything, including supervision of the family's many servants, cooking of meals, and many more details while her father managed the Fothergill business interests.

I shall not have many more days here, she reminded herself. *England can be lovely but no other place compares with this!*

For centuries, Alpine-fortified Switzerland had escaped being disturbed by blight of war, intrusion of disease any more serious than common colds, and other encroachments that invariably bedeviled the rest of Europe because all that was Swiss—the people as well as the land—seemed cut off from the rest of the European continent.

I seem still to have so much of this world left that I desire to travel, Clarice reminded herself. *I look forward to seeing Sicily, though news of some unruly and rather predatory element there is distressing. I hear that they hold the local citizens in terror and can never be tracked down by the authorities because everyone is afraid of running afoul of these crude and offensive men. Still, it is pleasing to the eyes, and I could hire some protection, I am sure.*

Destinations remained yet to seek and savor, like fruit on a tree, but not during this current trip, for she was planning to end it soon, drawn back to the countryside of Britain. Somehow, getting home had become increasingly important, but then, it was not an act of onerous deprivation to deny herself of any more foreign vistas that year since, at the age of twenty-two, Clarice had been able to enjoy more of the fruits of travel than most women during the whole of their lifetimes, until they were likely too old or ill or both to hit the roads or seaways any longer.

Most of the way, she had enjoyed what awaited her at each stop: the beauty and stark cleanliness of the Scandinavian countries; the ruggedness of Spain; the peaceful ancient forests of Bavaria. But Clarice was also very much a product of her upbringing, with all the "baggage" that entailed. Her inbred prejudices about the people of certain other countries were the same prejudices that had caused war in centuries past but which also gave way for arranged marriages that could further a political goal. She was especially resentful of the French. How their vanity angered Clarice, manifested by their incessant snootiness and a pervasive disdain that, by its nature, insulted most of the people of other nationalities that the average Frenchman would ever meet. And those Germans! The whole race seemed too cold and autocratic and demanding and, yes, militaristic for her tastes, though such thinking required her to forget the "glory days" of the British Empire and its many colonial outposts.

Since Clarice tried to enjoy the people of a country as much as the scenery, she found France and Germany to be less worthy of any further attention because of the characteristics of the citizens. On their next trip the year after their current stay in Switzerland, however, she was looking forward to spending some time in Rome which she understood to be the most fascinating of all European cities.

Why are we being drawn back home so suddenly? Clarice asked herself, her thoughts returning to that final evening before they left. . .

For a number of years, the sisters jetted off to Europe as the start of a family tradition: Their summer vacation lasted from mid-June through the first week of September. Wisely it had been their parents' way of helping them gain insights about life from the varied experiences both would undergo. While crossing France by automobile, with its many villages and lush countryside, to reach Switzerland, the sisters sometimes detoured south around the western end of the Alps, on down to the quaint northern region of Italy, then east through to Austria, and, finally, back up north again until they had crossed over into the eastern part of the Alps.

But on that final evening before they were driven to Heathrow Airport, Elizabeth Fothergill could not shake the sense of gloom that had overtaken her, no matter how much Clarice in particular tried to reassure her.

"It is the same now as before," the younger woman began. Elizabeth, who once had been rather plump of hip and stomach and boundlessly energetic, radiating a smile that showed itself readily and a voice that always seemed to be on the verge of lilting song, listened raptly. "Look, Mother, you should relax and not be so concerned. I wish you would conserve your strength. That would please Sarah and me very much, you know."

Clarice was uncomfortable reassuring her mother in this

fashion since doing so represented such a dramatic change in their relationship, a change that, months earlier, would have seemed impossible. But the passage of those months had changed their lives irreparably, it seemed, plunging Elizabeth Fothergill into a physical nightmare that she never expected to escape, and draining weight from her once robust body.

"I love you dearly but you may be very wrong," Elizabeth Fothergill replied finally but with no harshness. "Those visions I have. . .sometimes at night as the darkness surrounds me but not with any kind of comfort or peace, you know. . .sometimes as I am sitting outside, cared for by devoted helpers, my eyes closed, my mind drifting. . .these tell me otherwise, speaking of horrible events to come."

"From nothing?" twenty-year-old Sarah asked, with some concern that her mother's mind was finally being affected by her illness or the treatment their doctors had chosen. "Could you be imagining all this? You are so ill, with so many drugs in you. Don't you think that they could be the cause?"

Elizabeth shook her head emphatically.

"No, my dear, it is more real!" she exclaimed. "I get a sense of what I have told you as I spend time at my computer, my unease confirmed by others who have accessed the Internet, not just sick older women like me. I detect it in the quite young as well, adolescents who seem to have given up all hope for whatever reason. Without hope, they are being driven to peculiar pursuits. Remember what I told you earlier."

Sarah shivered as her mother spoke, recalling well those few minutes of conversation, minutes that seemed as chilling as the touch of a demon's cold hand on her shoulder. Had these thoughts originated because of a computer?

After Elizabeth had been confined to bed, or at least her wheelchair, she was given a Pentium 166 laptop computer, much more powerful than her old 486 model, her family hoping that dabbling in the Internet would be a worthwhile way for her to spend time that might otherwise have been wasted. They had found several Christian web pages, including one that had a superb on-line Bible study course.

"It is fascinating!" Elizabeth had exclaimed happily, a bit of color returning to her face, as she continued her "web-surfing." "Why, I can shop for clothes, perfume, hair spray, cakes and candies, and a tinful of those delicious pistachio nuts that I like so much. Almost anything I need is available with so little effort. If I were stronger, I could book theater tickets and plan a night out all from my laptop!"

That was the more resilient Elizabeth speaking, the one who seemed undaunted by any crisis. But as months slipped by, and her weight plummeted, with the level of pain and general discomfort escalating, she became less cheerful and more moody, her periods of depression increasing in length and severity.

Such morose behavior synchronized with her discoveries of the darker side of the Internet, including electronic chat rooms that were havens for misfits of every variety, such as pedophiles and rapists, pornographers, and even thinly disguised serial killers. She needed no further confirmation of the Internet's evil dimension when she read a front page newspaper story some weeks later that involved a teenaged girl who had fallen in love with someone via e-mail on the Internet, and was enticed to travel some distance to meet him at a predetermined rendezvous point. They ran away together and, gradually, he got her involved in the world of pimps and prostitutes, which ultimately drove her to suicide through an overdose of pills.

"But that isn't all," Elizabeth told her husband, Cyril, as well as her daughters during that period when the darkness was asserting itself. "I actually found detailed plans to create pipe bombs just by accessing the appropriate web site. Places where guns could be bought on the black market, where drugs are available for bargain prices, and the list doesn't end with these." She was quite terrified as she spoke.

"The Web has allowed me to see into utter damnation," Elizabeth continued. "Just yesterday I stumbled across a chat room set up for teenaged vampires! Think of that! Out of curiosity, assuming it was a promotion for some horror film, I accessed that site, and left after less than a minute. Even in that short period of time, I saw what could only be described as an outpost of hell itself!"

Her tone of urgency increased even as her voice trembled. Feeling a wave of nausea about to engulf her, she stopped talking briefly and, when the "spell" passed, she went on, though sounding weaker than before. "But it is the subtler flow of evil that is actually the more terrifying."

"What do you mean, Mother?" Sarah had asked.

"Something quite powerful is loose at this time," Elizabeth went on. "I could call it a malaise but it goes beyond that, actually."

And now, later, on the eve of her daughters' departure for the continent, her outlook apparently had not changed, which made her all the more vulnerable emotionally.

"But surely God wants you to look to Him, Mother," Clarice observed, unaware of the mistake she was making, "not strange, melancholy phantoms or cryptic Internet ravings!"

Abruptly, Elizabeth reached up and wrapped her fragile fingers around her daughter's wrist.

"I have known the Lord far longer than you!" she exclaimed with an indignation that did not have to be turned on for the occasion. "Perhaps you can bring yourself to believe that I have some measure of wisdom in such matters."

They were sitting on sturdy wooden chairs, made from the labors of a previous generation, in the middle of a small plot of earth cut out of the rolling lawn, a magnificent sea of green which stretched on for many miles in all directions. A thick, grayish morning mist hung over healthy trees that were abundant on the Fothergills' long-held land.

Earlier in her life, Lady Elizabeth Fothergill had not

been a woman given to any sudden outbursts of wild imaginings. Her levelheadedness was one of her finest traits. In fact, she seemed ever the most practical member of that family, for many years running a large household with efficiency, what with two daughters and more than thirty full-time servants, and a husband who was, in some respects, like other men who had grown up with wealth surrounding them.

Fiercely devoted to his loved ones, and respectful of his wife, Cyril Fothergill shunned the extramarital "activities" that would ensnare not a few others. But, however unconsciously, he relegated Elizabeth to that confining domestic role she handled so well, while he was off with other rich businessmen, planning a new purchase of property or selling an existing one. He spent much time trying to perceive properly whatever political wind of the moment happened to be blowing across the face of his world, and adjusting his various interests accordingly.

But that was before illness struck her down. . . .

Abruptly Clarice felt a hand on her shoulder.

"Sarah!" Clarice nearly yelled as she saw her sister standing next to her. "You about startled me out of my skin!"

"When I went to your room, I saw that you were up early today," the frail-looking twenty year old told her. "Usually I beat you by an hour."

Clarice smiled as she replied, "The closer I get to the day we are to leave, the more restless I am. I wish we could stay here for the rest of our lives."

"It does have everything but one. . .any good-looking young men. I have not seen anyone under the age of forty and most seem to be fifty or more. We have gone many miles in every direction but that is all we ever see, middle-aged, pot-bellied—"

Sarah blushed in midsentence.

"Forgive me," she said earnestly. "That is hardly a very pleasant or sanctified attitude, I know."

Clarice admired the courage and stamina that kept Sarah going through illness after illness. From persistent simple colds, blinding headaches, and nausea to muscle spasms and chest pains, Sarah, throughout her short life, frequently required special attention by Fothergill family physicians.

"But I feel so strong," Sarah had told her during one recent headache episode. "I can lift heavy pieces of furniture. I can—"

"Shush!" Clarice replied sympathetically. "You never have to explain anything to me. I accept you as my sister unconditionally, whether you are well or ill. Nothing you are, nothing you could say or do would end our relationship."

"But I want you to be proud of me!" Sarah exclaimed. "You must not feel that you are saddled with a weakling who is going to drag you down with her."

"I could never think that!" protested Clarice. "Mother and Father love you. And so do I, Sarah. You are very special to us. Please, you mustn't forget that."

It was not the first time they had had a discussion of that sort. Sarah's insecurities cropped up periodically.

"What is it that has disturbed you this time?" Clarice asked, trying to be as patient as always, but also feeling some weariness after so many years of being forced to confront the emotions that bedeviled her sister periodically.

Sarah seemed reluctant to answer.

"We have no secrets," Clarice reminded her.

"The village yesterday. . . ."

"What about it?"

"While you stayed in the chalet, I took out the Mercedes we rented in Paris for the drive here, and went into the village you and I both like so greatly, where I bought some things for the trip back home, you know, gifts for Mother and Father, and anything else that might catch my eye. I needed to do this today because of an uneasiness that I started feeling, to get my mind off it as much as possible."

Clarice assumed that her sister was surrendering to one

of those frequent dark moods of hers, making her so much like their mother of recent months.

"I see nothing so strange thus far," she said reassuringly. "Perhaps you are simply being—"

"No!" exclaimed Sarah, stepping back a bit from the wooden railing around the balcony on that side of the little chalet. "It is more than you imagine."

She bit her lower lip.

"Speak up," Clarice told her. "We are sisters, after all. You need never be afraid of my reaction, Sarah, never."

"On the way into the village I heard something over the radio," Sarah continued, her eyes half-closed as she recalled what it was, the chill she had felt as the newscaster delivered his bulletin, interrupting a radio concert by Domingo, Carreras, and Pavarotti.

"What was it about?"

"Some business regarding the Internet."

Clarice chuckled despite herself, notably unimpressed by that so-called revelation. "Is that all?"

Sarah shot her sister a look that Clarice knew all too well.

"Something is happening. . .something quite awful," she said. "I can't make light of it just yet but it's there, Clarice, just as Mother said, the beginning of—"

"If there were something bad," her sister interrupted, "you can be sure that someone would've phoned us or sent a messenger somehow. But we've heard nothing. Surely you aren't beginning to let Mother's fears afflict you as well."

Sarah shook her head.

"It's not that at all," she said. "According to the news report, it's just started. Perhaps Mr. Prindiville hasn't heard."

Her eyes widened as she felt a touch of anger, before adding defiantly, "After all, dear sister, this was a news *bulletin.*"

Clarice let the sarcasm pass.

"*What* has just started?" Clarice asked.

"Some subversive action," Sarah replied, her right cheek beginning to twitch slightly, another characteristic of hers when she was confronting something dire.

"You surely aren't serious."

"It *is* what I heard. And I detected no chuckling by the newscaster."

"Where did he say that this subversion is happening?"

"Across the United States and just now in Europe."

"*Here?* The Americans seem to be an increasingly lawless bunch but surely not in England or here?"

Clarice was conveniently ignoring the rash of bombings in London two years ago.

"Yes, *here!*" Sarah retorted. "I'm afraid that I can only say yes. Remote islands in the South Pacific perhaps may be unaffected for a while, but it appears that everywhere else madness is going to start, if it hasn't already."

"So suddenly? We live in an age of instant communication. Wouldn't we have heard some clues before now?"

"How often have you and I used the laptop lately?" Sarah reminded her. "How often have we turned on the radio or watched television? We have been outside, remember? In this glorious place, watching the birds, sniffing in the sweet air, talking with other young women well into the night!"

Clarice had to admit that her sister was speaking sensibly.

"But who could be responsible?" she mused.

"The authorities think some Islamic terrorist group."

"Bombs?" Clarice said nervously. "They couldn't be engaging in hand-to-hand combat, at least not in the U. S."

"None of that."

"What then?" Clarice asked as a look of terror settled on her face.

"Plague. A world-wide outbreak of what they are calling the Hanta virus, with those contracting it dying within twenty-four hours."

Clarice had been preparing herself to ridicule anything but that.

"Dear God!" she exclaimed not profanely.

"At first, just a few days ago, various governmental officials thought that canisters were being used."

"Dropped from airplanes?"

"And transported by boats rendezvousing with undercover agents in a dozen countries," Sarah added.

"But they were wrong, isn't that what you're going to tell me? It is being done some other way, right?"

Sarah was trembling and could only nod.

"Tell me the rest, please," Clarice implored her sister.

"Rats," Sarah managed to say, "infected rats are everywhere. It's been going on for weeks, gaining momentum by the day, first a case or two here and there, in places where it might be expected, India, the Philippines, the Sudan."

"So nobody thought much of it? Is that why we've heard nothing officially? Is there a news blackout? One that a single brave newscaster has decided to violate?"

"That's apparently the case, Clarice. Which I think is bad judgment on the part of the various governments. If this plague business is real, if it's actually in progress now, think of what that could mean. It's insidious. Evil by its nature. And very, very clever, so clever that it was impossible to detect until the plague spread to places that weren't so poverty-stricken, where the sewer systems were cutting-edge, I guess you could say."

They were silent for a few minutes, the scope of what Sarah had learned sinking in on both of them.

"Hundreds of thousands of rats," Sarah said finally, "breeding and producing millions more, and tens of millions in the next stage. Eventually hundreds of millions of disease carriers could be overrunning the whole world. And that's not counting the human carriers, the tourists, the diplomats, the business community."

Clarice studied the expression on Sarah's pale thin face, an expression that went beyond simple idle fear.

"A foul thing is in the air," Sarah continued. "It is ugly,

and yes, it is evil. It enters the body and in a few hours there
is death, Clarice, awful death, not just a quiet fading away, the
eyes closing, the heart ceasing to beat but an anguish over the
body from head to foot, not a single inch left unconsumed.
But it's worse than the plague that destroyed so much of the
population of Europe more than 600 years ago. There may be
no way to combat it, Clarice, no way at all! According to the
radio report, it is mutagenic, which means its characteristics
are constantly changing."

At that, she buried her face in her hands and Clarice
rushed to hug her thin body. Suddenly her sister pushed her
away.

"Sometimes you understand everything about me," she
said. "Other times you understand nothing."

Clarice was sorry about this, and asked Sarah to forgive
her.

"Of course I shall."

"All of this sounds so bizarre. It is hard for me to grasp
it all. Could the reports be exaggerated?"

"No," Sarah told her.

"How can you be sure?"

"I saw someone die of it yesterday."

"You saw—"

The man had seemed a bit younger than either of them.
He was staggering as he walked and coughing quite violently. People in the town square stood, seemingly paralyzed, and looked at him dumbly, either not knowing what
to do, or not wanting to do anything, for such diseases as
leprosy and others that caused an unusual appearance or
behavior were greeted with fear, fear that prevented even
decent people from trying to help.

"There were many villagers standing around," Sarah
recalled, trembling. "Yet he seemed to notice no one except
me."

He had stopped for a moment, his gaze locked on her,
like a master archer preparing to take aim.

"I. . .I cannot say why," she continued. "I just know how that man looked, all the pain of the world in those eyes of his, eyes that were blood red."

Her sister's palms were wet.

"Did he. . .touch you?"

Sarah bowed her head.

"Yes. . . ."

That was a moment she would never forget, one that seemed to freeze the full length of her body.

"I could feel those fingers of his touch the back of my hand for but a second or two." Sarah spoke slowly. "They were so cold, Clarice, the coldest flesh I. . .I have ever encountered. . .as though the poor soul were dead already."

A corpse. . .he appeared to be a walking corpse to her, moving, but no longer alive.

"I have never touched a dead body before, you know, but I imagine that that is how it does feel. . .*life gone, Clarice, life banished forever, only a lump of cold meat left!*"

Sarah hugged herself, shivering violently from that memory, fresh and ugly and scary as it was.

"I backed away. He continued toward me. I heard him utter a single name. He said, 'Baldasarre. . . .' And then he repeated it."

"Was that all?" Clarice asked.

"Only a few more words were spoken. After he said, 'Baldasarre. . . .' and just as he was falling to the ground at my feet, that poor, poor creature looked up into my eyes and muttered, 'Baldasarre serves only one master. . .the unholy Lucifer. . .Prince of Darkness. . .*beware!*'

"Suddenly some people burst out from an alleyway and grabbed this man quite roughly, and then dragged him away. He was screaming, coughing up blood. It was so ghastly to see him."

"But why did they treat him so cruelly?"

Clarice waited, gritting her teeth in preparation for any new shock.

"He was a Jew. . . ," Sarah added. "I know because he was wearing that little round cap, you know, on the back of his head."

The two young women stood on the brightly colored balcony without speaking for several minutes.

"All that you saw and heard seems so distant here. . . now. . .in this place. . . ," Clarice said wistfully.

Sarah perked up at that.

"We could stay longer," she suggested tentatively.

She was not accustomed to venturing very much of anything in such situations, preferring to let Clarice take over as usual. Now a bit of color was showing in her cheeks as the adrenaline started to flow at the prospects ahead of them.

"We could avoid the town altogether, you know, raise whatever food you and I would need right here. This valley is not well-known. It's hidden well enough. We might be as safe here as anywhere else, for a while, anyway."

Turning slightly, Sarah caught a glimpse of the rear of the family's sprawling property, of the simple, beautiful garden that Clarice and she had started, mostly as a pleasant hobby instead of out of anything resembling necessity, with some lettuce, string beans, onions, leeks, and other vegetables.

It did not seem like something too lowly, Clarice thought. *We've enjoyed doing this, raising food ourselves instead of having to depend upon the labors of others.*

Back home, at the family estate, doing any such manual work, with dirt actually getting under the fingernails, would have been considered unseemly, more appropriately left to the staff gardener. But this was not the case in the midst of this Swiss valley inhabited as it was by only a handful of wealthy men and women who, like Clarice and Sarah, were from England, and a few who were from Germany.

At the opposite end of the Fothergill property, up on a plateau some 2,000 feet or so above the valley's verdant floor, was a 300-year-old monastery with fewer than two dozen monks who devoted themselves in their splendid isolation to serving God. The valley seemed, at once, a place of the rich while, at the same time, one that took care of more spartan needs.

"There would be no meat as a rule, except on rare occasions," Sarah offered. "We could somehow hunt some pheasants, eat whatever else we could catch."

"The men might help us," Clarice suggested rather tentatively. "We could form a group perhaps."

"Lizards. . . ."

Sarah's reluctance in suggesting that particular source of food was apparent.

"Yes. . .if it meant continuing to live," Clarice agreed, with as little pleasure over the prospect as her sister displayed.

Continuing their cloistered lifestyle was clearly one of the better of a limited number of possibilities since nothing apparently had reached into the valley as yet. Their Swiss haven might serve to stand against anything.

"Oh, Lord. . . ," Clarice said prayerfully, her eyes closed.

Impulsively, she reached out toward her sister and took that familiar bony hand in her own, feeling a need for solace that only she could give.

"We must contact Mother and Father, tell them what we plan," she added, "Place a call, hope that it gets through."

"What about a quarantine?" Sarah asked. "The Swiss would not feel hesitant about forcing us to stay here for whatever time necessary."

"Even if they didn't," Clarice said, "the Germans, French, and Italians could impose a quarantine that would last far longer than we might be inclined to stay."

She was beginning to feel powerless, a gathering inevitability that seemed like a tidal wave ready to sweep over the two of them, as well as their parents, corrupting everything that they had ever known.

The sisters looked at the valley around them, at the

peaks crowned with glistening snow, and beyond, to the clouds above.

"Eden. . . ," Clarice mused, sighing. "So fine, so beautiful, tucked away just for you, just for me, it almost seems."

Sarah nodded, even as a chill gripped every nerve in her less than robust body. She wondered briefly if, somehow, she were being warned of a tragedy ahead.

Lord, Lord, she thought, the very notion unsettling, *are we to shiver each time someone knocks at the front door or whenever we hear a sudden sound in the middle of the night, like demons shrieking together in the darkness?*

Instinctively, she folded the fingers of both hands into fists, but without any anger. Back home, whenever she was afraid, she had done the same thing.

. . .our Eden, our peace, our joy.

Clarice and Sarah Fothergill suddenly found themselves wrestling with the same dread that had grabbed hold of their mother, one which they had scoffed at so openly. Now this dread was poking its unwanted way through the tranquillity of this valley so far away from home.

"How long will this place remain as it is?" Clarice sighed, an inexpressible sorrow overtaking her. But the most terrifying thought of all was left unspoken.

How soon the serpent. . .

CHAPTER 2

They stayed up late that night, hoping to get some news over their 27-inch television set. But there was nothing that seemed overt, except for little clues: an epidemic in a town in Spain that hadn't had one for centuries—the impression left was that it was strictly a localized outbreak, and a viral epidemic per se was never mentioned; an item about a clampdown on sales of rats destined to become pets in homes in a number of countries; and other rather mild-seeming reports which, individually, seemed harmless but taken together seemed a harbinger of the gathering nightmare.

Clarice and Sarah needed to get as much rest that night as they could manage since neither had any idea what the next few days would hold in store for them. But since both found it difficult to fall asleep right away, they stayed awake for some time, thinking back to three years earlier when the specter of tragedy was not threatening their lives. . .until that time their father made his urgent trip across Europe and on to the Vatican, that time, they could see in hindsight, was the true beginning of tribulation. . .

Even in the last decade of the twentieth century, Clarice and Sarah had had their lives built around the castle they called home, though they got away from it more often, faster, and at a greater distance than their medieval ancestors could ever manage.

Our castle. . .

At 600 feet, it was a structure of remarkable length even in a region of ancient massive fortress-homes, its battlemented walls shored up by several powerful towers which were, in some instances, square in shape and, in others, cylindrical. The stone that had been used to buildit originally as well as for additions over the centuries included gray limestone as well as yellow and dark red sandstone.

Gaining entry to the castle meant going through the imposing great gatehouse, a staple of such structures, which was situated at the eastern end. It led to a large grassy court-yard fully 170 feet square.

During medieval times, the staff in charge of maintain-ing the castle and performing various functions within included a wide range of individuals, men and women with specific duties: dispensers, cupbearers, fruiterers, a slaugh-terer, a baker, various cooks, a brewer, someone to look after the tablecloths, a wafer maker, a sauce cook, and a poulterer, each with a boy helper.

The chamberlain and a cofferer were responsible for the chests that contained money and silver cups, saucers, and spoons. The keeper of the wardrobe used tailors to make the family's clothing. A laundress washed the clothes, sheets, tablecloths, and towels.

But there were yet other members that comprised the staff, including a marshal who was in charge of the servants assigned to working in the stables: grooms, smiths, carters, and clerks.

Nor was the size of the combined groups of the staff unusual. If anything, the family seemed to be fairly mod-est in its need for staffers, in comparison to other lords then and in centuries past for whom the number of servants they had seemed a mark of their own worth as human beings.

In the modern England of the last decade of the twen-tieth century, the current Fothergill family had needs that were not as elaborate. A host of stores had been built near-by, including supermarkets, so no one had to go all the way to London just to get certain necessities.

Still the family had need to employ guards, the weary guards, who were required to protect many millions of dol-lars' worth of antiques, fine oil paintings, and a collection of jewels that would have made the queen more than a little jealous if she were ever to find out about them.

Most of these men were aging but still highly capable veteran members of the London police department, with a few from Scotland Yard, just eight of them, now largely spending their time rehashing memories of the sights and sounds of metropolitan detective work during which they investigated rapes, murders, robberies, terrorist provocations, and more, sometimes boring work, often unpleasant, but sometimes thrilling, giving them a surge of adrenaline.

Now serving "only" as guardians on the Fothergill estate, they were in the throes of acclimating themselves to the status of has-beens who yearned for the periodic excitement of the old days.

"We guarantee the safety of a single family, its possessions, and its servants," moaned one of the men. "We should be glad that we have any kind of employment, of course, but I yearn for the sound of cracking bones and the sight of blood running deep into the alleys of London."

They were now a bored lot, rather like aging actors who had passed out of favor with the public, but after being so well trained, and spending their lives in only one profession, they were ill-equipped to embrace any other pursuit.

"It hurts a great deal to be no longer adored by your country," Roger Prindiville, one of the older former bobbies, admitted as he and Cyril Fothergill were taking a walk along the western boundary of the family's property.

Prindiville's shoulders slumped.

"I feel so useless," he muttered, "with no more criminals to track down, all this training going to waste like a rusting suit of armor, and me along with it."

The reason Cyril had chosen to spend time with Roger Prindiville was that he had noticed the man on several occasions during the past two weeks not wearing his bobby's garb. Further, instead of hanging out with the others working for the Fothergills, he seemed to be staying by himself, hardly moving, or when he did, with unusual lethargy.

"You have no family, do you?" Cyril asked sympathetically, while knowing the answer. "Nor do any of your comrades."

"Most of us were not blessed with such loved ones but others were, and even with them, loneliness and despair returned because the ones who were married later found that their wives could not tolerate the pressures," Prindiville recounted. "They could not share themselves with the general public whose needs were insatiable."

"Good fortune has been with me and my loved ones all my life, dear man," Cyril acknowledged.

The exception he was not talking about was Raymond Fothergill, his father.

"You see, I have the very best wife any sensible man could possibly want. Elizabeth is truly one of God's greatest gifts. I thought that at the beginning of our marriage, and I have never been persuaded by anyone or anything to the contrary."

"You are blessed," the other man agreed. "But there is only one Lady Fothergill, and no other man can have her."

"And my daughters also—splendid girls those two, headstrong, yes, but honest and virtuous and reasonably consistent Christians."

"That they are. You have all that you could want, Lord Fothergill."

"Every man desires a son to carry on his heritage, but I could not be prouder of Clarice and Sarah."

"And I know that they love and admire you. I overhear them talking. They would die for you, sir, as you would die for them," Prindiville stated sincerely.

Cyril did not have to think long and hard before realizing why he liked this man.

As a morning mist still hung over the land, the two sisters shared a walk around a distant portion of the estate, though they were careful to carry a beeper in the event an emergency occurred.

"It is like the world being born again," Sarah said, sighing, "and this land is among the first brought to life by God."

Clarice had a reaction akin to that one.

"And we are among the first new human beings, you and I," she said as they walked briskly. "Listen to that, Sarah, listen!"

A particularly raucous-sounding bird seemed somehow to be calling only to the two of them.

"Another life born," Clarice said, smiling appreciatively. "I have heard that same sound all these years. I can not understand how this could be, but it is."

Just then a squirrel darted across their path.

"And another," Sarah added.

They saw in the hazy distance a wild horse running up one grass-covered slope and immediately down another.

"More of creation stirs," Sarah said, pointing, eyes wide, as that new thought made familiar surroundings come alive with meaning.

Another horse following the first one, and two more after that.

The sisters stopped briefly, inhaling the clean air.

"Father has never done this as far as I know," Sarah stated. "He has always maintained control of all the land for miles around, yet now he seems lost in details that have nothing to do with the beauty of it. How sad, Clarice, how sad."

"It is an enterprise to him," her sister replied. "It is as though the necessity of maintaining this estate has blinded him to what God has given him."

Sarah nodded in complete agreement.

"Grandfather has never been like that, you know," she recalled. "He is a bit ribald from time to time, less a Christian for his rapscallion ways, of course, but then he understands how precious is the joy of life itself and has lived every moment with zest."

She threw up her hands in exasperation.

"And there is our father, a fine man who seems every bit the stronger, more dedicated Christian of the two but, ironically, less appreciative of the blessings Almighty God has bestowed. It seems sometimes that he is working hard —to make sure that nothing can take away—what he has. If the Lord gives, the Lord can take away, and nothing Father does can prevent that from happening or so much as delay it for a bit."

Sarah paused, trying to choose words that conveyed precisely what she wanted Clarice to understand.

"In heaven," she went on, "which one will be given the greater blessings, Grandfather or Father? You would think it would be Father, wouldn't you?"

Clarice shook her head, catching the point her sister was trying to make.

"I wonder about that, Sarah," she remarked. "I do wonder about it more than you might realize. Is our father truly a better witness for the faith? He sees a sunrise and reacts little, and goes on to the business matters of the day. Grandfather, though, drops to his knees when there is an especially vivid one, muttering about the master Artist who flings an array of brilliant colors with such stunning effect, and he then thanks God for the blessing of that beautiful moment.

"Now if that is where it ended, we would not feel so frustrated, Sarah, for the answer would seem less obscure, with Grandfather clearly more useful to the Lord as a witness to others. But there he is, taking to his ale by evening, great quantities of it, his tongue loosened as a result, and the words falling from his mouth rather shamefully. And yet—"

"By morning, Grandfather is up with the sun," Sarah finished for her, "proceeding to speak a prayer that none of us could hope to match for its Christian fervor. Throughout the day, at different moments, he hums or sings songs of praise, treating people with charity and grace. . .until dusk comes. . . and that other side of him takes over, dark like the coming night itself."

Raymond Fothergill. . .

Capable of drinking anyone under the table, he was a man who embodied a lustful approach to life and Christianity that continually embarrassed the other members of his family, in particular his only child, Cyril.

Yet Raymond Fothergill, now well into his seventies, was without doubt a true follower of God. He never conquered the excesses of his sin nature, but for every observer who looked at him and scoffed, many others saw that other side of which his granddaughter Sarah spoke. A short time after Sarah and Clarice had enjoyed their morning walk, Raymond was assaulted by massive pains in his chest. Although much of his body was virtually paralyzed afterward, he was able to turn his head and move his right arm, and he could still talk, with nearly as much clarity as before.

"What does it all mean?" he asked one morning after breakfast in bed had been served to him by his granddaughters. "I have never been less than devoted to the blessed Savior. And yet I also have not been able to pass up a jug of ale or some wine imported from the south of France or anything else that was intoxicating."

He tried to chuckle but the pain that resulted made him stop.

"Shall I sin that grace abound all the more?" he repeated from Scripture. "At one time I think I deceived myself into believing that, you know. I became convinced that the greater the sin, the more startling the redemption would seem."

Raymond wiped away some tears that were slipping down his cheek.

"But after a riotous night at a nearby estate or a simple little tavern in the village yonder, I would come stumbling back here, feeling foolish, feeling guilt that I could never escape. It was as though I had to make it all up to the

Almighty by being more dedicated, by witnessing to more people who I prayed would not be aware of that other part of me, that other life I was leading, and be able to point their finger at me, and shout, 'Hypocrite! Hypocrite!' "

Raymond waved his one good arm about the room in which he soon would die.

"Look at the number of people who have stopped by to visit this castle because of my son's business. I was able to take them aside and, since many knew nothing about me, I could approach them most convictingly," he went on. "How many has it been? I never counted, you know. I just felt drawn to these people, eager to share with them the loving, forgiving Savior who was so dear to me."

"We have lost count, Grandfather," Sarah replied. "It was scores, or more. Yes, I would not be surprised if it were more than that."

He turned slightly and looked at her.

"I would like to touch your cheek," he told her. "Would you bend down just a bit, my dear?"

As he caressed her cheek, his fingers seemed a bit like those of a master sculptor examining with awe someone else's surpassing craftsmanship.

"So very beautiful," he told her, "so delicate. I fear that you might break under the weight of—"

An attack of coughing gripped him, his eyes rolling up in their sockets for a moment, and then it passed.

"I have misspent so many of the blessings that Father God has given me," he acknowledged. "And now my body is giving out. My strength is gone, and any hope for recovery along with it."

"But has not your son done the very same in another way?" Clarice countered wisely, without seeming overly critical.

Raymond looked strangely puzzled.

"As far as he is concerned," she explained, "expanding his fortune is the greatest of endeavors. And Father has so much on his mind these days that he appears, to my sister and me, and to others, a colorless man, someone almost without humanity."

Raymond Fothergill closed his eyes momentarily, giving Clarice and Sarah a start.

"You may be right, dear girl. I have been too busy over the years seeking my own amusement to pay a great deal of attention to what my son was doing."

"How could the two of you be so different?" Sarah asked.

"Cyril saw the extent of my multiplied excesses and determined he would not be like me."

It was a profoundly simple statement but one that was devastatingly honest.

"You spoke of how many people I have influenced for the Lord," he continued, "because, I suppose, people perceived me, in my lucid moments, as the 'nicer' of the brothers Fothergill. I had rosier cheeks, and I spoke heartily, and I could tell amusing stories. I smiled often, and I patted men on the back instead of merely shaking their hand. My eyes sparkled, and there was a jauntiness to my step."

He coughed but there was no blood.

"Have you thought, however, of how many people who were potential Christians continually turned their back on the faith because of me?" he asked, glancing from one to the other. "You learn of the ones who have taken me aside and inquired of Christ and whom I have been able to lead to the Lord, and that is fine, of course, but think of this, my beloved granddaughters: How great, can we guess, is that number of those who have seen the likes of the wretched Raymond Fothergill swilling down some intoxicating brew, eating to the point of utter gluttony, and perhaps consorting with a woman who was not my wife—may God rest that soul—and been disgusted by such displays of wantonly unsanctified living?"

His eyes showed some of his despair.

"Will there be a single moment before heaven closes around me when I shall see the damned looking right up at me from that foul, foul place, and pointing their fingers in accusation even as I am snatched from their sight and they must be resigned to the eternal flames?"

Raymond Fothergill smiled with some irony. The past few months of sickness and rising guilt over a tumultuous array of memories had taken a toll on his body, his former girth steadily evaporating until he was left emaciated and pale. Little did the sisters realize that their mother would look almost as ravished just two years later.

"There may be souls in heaven because of me," he said, "but I doubt that there are any in hell as a result of your father's conduct."

Clarice understood what her grandfather was saying, but she still could not overlook what seemed so wrong with the way her father had been living his life.

"But Father conducts himself sternly most of the time," Clarice offered. "He seems so very—"

"Unloving? Is that it?"

"Yes. . . ."

"Yet you know that he does love you."

"We can guess that by actions only we are able to see," Clarice said. "But what about those on the outside, the great many people who see only the apparent coldness, the absence of—"

"I know, I know," Raymond interrupted. "You need not repeat yourself. Have you considered that a decision for Christ that seems lost may only be one that is delayed for the present, for whatever reason the blessed Savior has in mind? He defends Himself to no one, you know, especially the likes of me. And have you confronted something else, that the timing may be His and His alone?"

Clarice and Sarah had heard their grandfather talk many times like that to outsiders. Occasionally, they went with him to London and stayed for a few days at Windsor Castle, the royal family's chief residence since the reign of William the Conqueror nearly 400 years earlier. Sometimes, when they awakened after sunrise and could not get back to sleep, both took to wandering through the castle's long, dark hallways. It was hardly a rare occasion when they would hear their grand-father talking to one or two of the servants and once or twice to Prime Minister Harold Edling himself, presenting the plan of salvation with great clarity. Later, as Raymond's "short-comings" became known to his granddaughters, they found it confusing to try and reconcile two images so completely disparate—the dedicated missionary for Christ that their grandfather seemed so often and the drunkard who was out of control.

"It is a war," he had told them a few years before, "the flesh against the spirit, and the spirit against the flesh. When I know what I should do, I end up doing that which I should not. Sometimes God's Spirit dwelling within me wins out over my sin nature, but the rest of the time it is those unholy impulses that gain the control."

That impression stayed with Clarice and Sarah during the years to follow. A few hours after breakfast, as they saw Raymond Fothergill on what would prove to be his death-bed, it was clear that he had finally won that war.

"The Scriptures say that in heaven there shall be an absence of all weeping and sorrow and pain, which afflicted us when we were in the flesh," he told them, his eyes glis-tening. "I take that to mean that everything in the past that was dirty and shameful will be gone. We will have a fresh slate, one that will remain clean for eternity."

Clarice and Sarah only listened to what their grandfather was telling them, while trying very hard not to break down in front of him. Abruptly, he sat up straight in bed and then he fell back, exhausted.

"Send my son in to see me," he demanded. "I shall have to talk with him before it is too late and eternity stills my voice. He must realize that enjoying life and letting others see his delight will not cause him to become like his wretched old father, a sodden embarrassment to the rest of the family."

Becoming weaker by the hour, Raymond bravely continued speaking.

"I must beg Cyril to forgive me for making him run so completely in the opposite direction all these years."

He looked from Clarice to Sarah, guilt written over his face.

"Is my flesh and blood here now?" he asked.

"No," Sarah told him. "Father is in London on business. We are not sure when he will return."

The disappointment Raymond felt seemed to take shape, distorting his face for an instant.

"Then I shall have to go to my knees and stay there," he announced, "begging the Lord to send my son back to me before I pass through the vale."

"No, Grandfather, you must lie down," Sarah protested. "If you conserve your strength, then you might—"

"That Spirit of the living God who dwells within me shall be my strength, child," he told her warmly. "Help me out of this bed, or I shall waste some of that supposedly unfailing strength you speak of trying to do it all by myself."

Clarice did as he had asked.

"Thank you, dear, dear girls," Raymond said, gasping, as he clasped both hands together and bowed his white-maned head. "Now leave me to these moments so precious between the Father and myself."

The two sisters left and walked down the hallway, intending to go downstairs but stopping instead at the landing.

"I could feel so many bones," Sarah said, close to sobbing.

"He is nearly gone," Clarice added with mounting sadness. "I think he may be dead by morning."

"We have to tell Mother," Sarah advised. "We have to get everybody ready. Someone must go to the mortician, the—the—"

As they started down the stairs, Clarice took her sister's hand, attempting to calm her.

"He will *die* like that," Sarah said. "We have to go back and put him in bed, make him comfortable."

"Let him do what he wants," Clarice said calmly. "Can we not give him the privilege of dying on his knees as he offers up a prayer?"

"You are so strong, so solid. I usually let my emotions rule me, and this hardly ever turns out well. Is that why I feel as deeply as I do about what is going on with Grandfather? Are not he and I just a little alike?"

"And perhaps I can be compared with Father. Is that what you are saying?"

"He is a wonderful man. Does that bother you?"

"Of course not. I was just realizing how different you and I are, and yet how close we have become over the years."

In such a household, preparing for death would not be a small enterprise. Both sisters realized they had to get started immediately.

"Just let me put my ear to the door," Sarah said with a firmness that could not be shaken. "I need to hear him."

Clarice nodded, and her sister scampered back down the hallway, pausing at the closed door. She held her breath, knowing that his voice would be weak, and she surely would have to strain to hear him. Without making a sound, Sarah motioned frantically for Clarice to rejoin her.

Hurry! her lips seemed to be saying.

Together the two of them pressed up tightly against the door and listened, astonished, at the strong voice that was praying vibrantly within the room.

"How can that be?" Sarah whispered. "Our grandfather is, as we have seen, at the door of death just as surely as you and I stand before this one. How could he be speaking so firmly. . .and with such sweet joy?"

Both were tempted to open the door and peer inside. But they resisted, granting their grandfather the privacy that he yearned for during the final moments of his life. By the time they reached the first floor, they could still hear faintly behind them the anguished sounds of an old man praying with great fervor for the son he loved to return before angels arrived as his shepherds to heaven.

When Clarice and Sarah confided in their mother a short while later, she knew that there could be no mistake. Although she trusted their judgment, and seldom questioned it, nonetheless, she could only act dumbfounded.

"If you knew even a few of the many stories about my father-in-law," Elizabeth said rather distantly.

"We have heard enough to make us see the contrast between our father and our grandfather," Clarice said.

"I used to think that the worse Raymond became, the more 'proper' Cyril seemed dedicated to becoming," she mused, "and at first I saw nothing unfortunate or wrong about that. The reputation of the family was at stake."

She sighed as she added, "How we learn, how we learn!"

"Grandfather wants to see Father as soon as he returns," Sarah told her. "He is praying that this will be so."

"I can only think that prayer cannot but do him good."

Sarah lowered her voice.

"On his knees!" she went on.

"His knees?" her mother exclaimed. "How could you have allowed that?"

"It was what he wanted," Clarice said.

"But he will faint. And he could hurt himself by falling on his side and breaking a rib or hitting his head!"

They were standing outside the kitchen area.

Immediately Elizabeth started toward the stairs. Half-way up when she stopped, she raised the fingers of her left hand to her mouth and gasped loudly enough for Clarice and Sarah to hear her.

In seconds they were at her side.

"Mother, are you all right?" they asked at the same time.

"Listen. . ." she said.

Grandfather Fothergill was yet praying, his voice sounding the strongest in some months.

"How can someone his age be so strong?" Elizabeth asked in a hushed voice.

"I think that the Lord is giving Grandfather the strength he will need until Father returns home," Sarah said wisely.

The three of them knew that there could be no other explanation.

"And return he will, of course, but in time only if my husband forgets for once his penchant for pinning down every detail of whatever business transaction he happens to be handling while away," Elizabeth remarked nervously. "That, my daughters, is too big an *if* for me to feel at all comfortable until he returns."

The next few hours passed with great tension as they waited for Cyril to return from London. Elizabeth, Clarice, and Sarah took turns stopping by those long, curving, stone stairs, waiting to hear the sound of Raymond's voice. Sometimes it seemed weaker, then stronger, then weaker, but they heard it in any event. Seven hours later, Elizabeth decided that something had to be done, whether Raymond agreed or not.

"We must get him off his knees and back in bed," she told her daughters. "The Lord never condones foolishness. He counsels us to be wise, to be vigilant, to be cautious even in our well doing. We must not forget this."

They had to agree with her, and both loved her all the more for that display of wisdom.

"Let us help you, Mother," Clarice said.

"I will *need* you," she said.

And they followed her upstairs. The voice seemed like a beacon, pulling them forward. Finally they hesitated as they stood before the door.

"Look!" Clarice said as she pointed toward the floor.

Light. Brilliant light. Its colors forming a rainbow at their feet.

Gasping, Elizabeth swung open the door and they entered the room to face a tableau that could never be forgotten. Raymond Fothergill was no longer on his knees.

"How did you—" Elizabeth struggled to find the words.

He was sitting up in bed, his arms outstretched, reaching—

For a creature clothed in iridescence!

Clarice's mouth opened, then closed again, and no words were spoken.

"Mother. . . ," Sarah said.

Then they heard from below noises, shouts. Alarmed, the three of them swung around. Someone was rushing up the stairs.

A male servant turned the corner and ran toward the three of them, yelling, "Lord Cyril, milady! Lord Cyril has finally returned!"

Hearing this, Raymond faced the doorway, that simple movement requiring great effort.

"My son, my son!" he whispered hoarsely, his eyes open wide. "Praise Jesus!"

Then he spoke again, not to Elizabeth, Clarice, or Sarah, but to the other presence in that room.

"I must be with Cyril," he pleaded. "Please, I beg You, let me linger just a short while longer. Please, please, dear Heavenly Father, let me do that. I ache for that new body You have promised. But how can I go just yet, knowing how little joy my son has when I shall be embracing so much of it for eternity?

"If I should die, O Lord, without spending this final moment of mortality alone with him, my son will have to ask himself over and over, 'If only I had arrived sooner.' I know Cyril so intimately, how he would torture himself. *Please. . . that should not happen, Father God!*"

That form in the room shimmered once, twice, a third time, and seemed to nod before it disappeared. Darkness prevailed again, broken only by the unsteady light from a single candle on an oval wooden table next to the bed.

"Stay here with him," Elizabeth told her daughters. "I will go and fetch your father immediately."

The servant joined her as she hurried downstairs.

"Did you see it?" Raymond asked as his granddaughters sat down on the ancient bed.

They both nodded.

"I felt so clean when it was here," he told them, "so pure. It was as though I had never sinned at all. Can you understand that? All those filthy caprices were as old clothes, flung aside but much more than that, *wiped out!*"

Perspiration formed on his forehead.

"The pain. . ." Raymond muttered, his voice strained. "The terrible pain. . .in. . .in my stomach, my bowels. . .eaten away as they are by what I used to guzzle down my throat . . .I have no fight left in me. . .my beloved. . .this battered body is collapsing, collapsing rapidly and. . .and it hurts. . . how greatly it hurts."

He held onto their hands.

"Stay, dear ones. Stay with me until my Cyril, my beloved Cyril, comes back. I. . .I simply cannot face being alone just now. There are other *things* in this room as we speak, you know, the most unholy beings, mocking me, shouting into my very soul the worst obscenities."

He pulled away and pressed his hands over his ears. "They are trying to say that I only imagined that beautiful form, and they want me to believe that it was nothing more than what I desperately wanted to see before I died. Tell. . . tell these evil creatures that you saw it, too. . .that it thrilled your own souls. *Tell them that!*"

Clarice and Sarah thought their grandfather was merely rambling as death approached, that he could not know what he was saying, and so they kept silent out of respect for him.

"I know how that must sound," Raymond acknowledged as he saw their expressions. "I can see what you must be thinking. But it is true. I cannot reach out and touch them. I can only sense their presence, their cold, cold forms.

"They want to steal me away from heaven, their kind does. They want to take old Raymond Fothergill screaming to the very gates of hell, treating my redemption as a will o' the wisp fantasy, destroyed by the flames of perdition."

The two sisters tried to be respectful, patting him gently on the shoulder while muttering reassuring platitudes, pretending that they wholly accepted what he was telling them. Raymond, however, could tell that they did not and, knowing this, fell back against the bed, defeat showing on his face.

"I cannot last another moment," he whispered. "Take me, Lord, quickly, take me beyond the reach of the enemies of my soul who seem so close, so—"

Raymond's chest was barely moving, his fingers closing into fists, then opening again, relaxing.

"I think I am being called to the dear Savior," he said, barely audibly. "Good-bye, my dear beloved ones."

His eyes started to close.

"Father!" a voice shouted.

Standing in the doorway, Cyril Fothergill hurried over to the bed in that sparsely furnished little room, dropped to his knees, and gently took his father's left hand between both of his own.

"I came as soon as I was told," he explained, breathing heavily, betraying more emotion than anyone had seen in a long time. "I would not have left if I had suspected that you were—"

Cyril then started crying. No member of his family had ever seen him cry, but now the flow of tears was steady, and some touched his father's own cheeks as they slipped from his jaw. Raymond's eyes opened with obvious great effort.

"My son, my son, it is you!" he exclaimed hoarsely. "I heard your voice as though from a great distance. I called out to you, Cyril, but you could not hear me."

He swallowed a couple of times, his throat very dry.

"I did not want to let my son go. I held onto your voice

as though it were a rope across some dark chasm before I reached the gates to eternity. It pulled me back, Cyril, it pulled back me but only for a short while, I am afraid. Only—"

His pale, lined face smiled with a transcendent peace that they all would reflect upon for many days afterward. Raymond Fothergill glanced first at Elizabeth, and then at the two grandchildren he had loved all their lives.

"I. . .love you. . .all," he told them warmly, his voice trembling. "But I must be alone now with this my blessed son. . .I seek his forgiveness. . .and that is a private matter between us."

Elizabeth and Clarice kissed Raymond on the forehead and hurried out of the room without turning to cast a glance behind them. Only Sarah turned as she shut the door, and was rewarded with a scene for which she long had been praying.

With momentarily renewed strength, Raymond Fothergill had managed to reach up and was folding his pale, bony arms around Cyril as sobs overtook father and son. Minutes later, an angel of light reentered that ancient room and took the old man's soul on his last journey, a solitary one as it commenced, but ending as eternity's choir welcomed him with jubilant hosannas, shorn as he finally was of his many sins, and a proud Heavenly Father embracing him at last.

The funeral of Raymond Fothergill drew hundreds of people from every region of the British Isles and several countries of Europe. Testimonies of his kindness, which seemed bent on poking through the scoundrel side of his nature, went on literally for hours.

The homeless came to pay their respects as well. A special contingent of poor men, women, and children was bused in from London, every last one of them having had some contact with Raymond.

Finally, after Raymond was buried on a portion of the estate reserved for the deceased of many centuries, and a memorial banquet held, Elizabeth and her daughters, tired from the supervision of this massive event, headed upstairs to their respective bedrooms.

Elizabeth heard her husband gasp, an unusual reaction for a man like him, and she looked over her shoulder. Just then she heard him say, "We must talk in the library. I trust my people but there should be only your ears and mine on this one."

Cyril was talking to one of his closest friends, Lord Alfred Hatterley. Elizabeth, who knew well her husband's moods, nearly lost her footing and tumbled down the stairs as she detected evidence of his state of mind. Something was afoot that was ten times more shocking than the death of his father.

Elizabeth saw the solemn expression on Cyril's face as he sensed her standing on the stairs and looked up.

"Do not wait up for me," he told her. "I shall be going to the library, and I cannot say how long I need to remain there."

"Are you all right?" Elizabeth asked in concern, raising her normally soft voice.

"Please trust my judgment. It is a terribly serious matter."

He threw her a kiss and then Hatterley and he proceeded down the hallway to the library.

Elizabeth could hear Cyril grunting as he opened the library's heavy wooden door. Concerned, she walked up the stairs, wondering if the inspiring mood of that evening was entirely transitory, shimmering brightly for a time, and then gone save for the memory of it, leaving no life-changing legacy.

When Cyril did not come upstairs to bed by midnight, Elizabeth grew more concerned. She waited for as long as she was able to restrain herself then hurried downstairs. One of the household staff met her at the bottom step, a young woman named Anne, tall, thin-faced, and not many years older than Clarice.

"Have you seen my husband?" Elizabeth inquired,

trying not to betray any anxiety.

"Lord Fothergill is still in the library," Anne replied. "I was just coming up to knock at your door, milady."

Elizabeth's eyes widened, despite her attempt at self-control.

"Why?" she asked, alarmed. "Have you reason to suspect anything is wrong?"

Anne grimaced because she, like the other servants, was genuinely fond of Elizabeth, and abhorred any prospect of upsetting her.

"I heard Lord Fothergill praying very loudly, and, just moments ago, he seemed to be in some distress."

"I shall go to my husband right away," Elizabeth told her. "Thank you, Anne."

She nearly ran down the hallway. Upon reaching the door, Elizabeth pressed her ear against it but could hear nothing at first. And then she pushed on it.

Locked. From the other side.

"Cyril!" Elizabeth called in to him. "I must know if you are all right. Speak to me, my dearest."

A number of seconds passed but there was no immediate reaction from within the library.

Lord, Lord, she prayed to herself, *please intercede here. I need Thee this hour.*

She waited, calling to Cyril one more time. Then, finally, Elizabeth heard the sound of movement inside, a chair being pushed back, a clearing of the throat, footsteps. The door was slowly opened, flickering candlelight reflected on the left side of her husband's head.

"I *am* sorry," he told her after she had walked in and confronted him. Hatterley had already left.

"What has come upon you so suddenly?" Elizabeth asked.

Cyril turned away, not eager to be as forthright as he usually was with his wife. Long ago they had decided that one part of the foundation of their marriage would be their agreement to express unyielding candor.

"Alfred felt compelled to tell me something before he left," Cyril said cryptically. "He wanted this to be in confidence, but he suspected that I would tell you anyway. We must not, however, let Clarice and Sarah know."

"But what could possibly upset you so much?"

Cyril faced Elizabeth again.

"The very real likelihood that someday you and I and our daughters might lose everything this family has had for generations."

He gestured about that room.

"Ashes at our feet, beloved. . .mere ashes through which we stumble numbly."

Elizabeth stepped back, stunned that he would say that.

"You have had *everything* in your family for centuries," she said. "So have I, Cyril, through my mother and my father, dating back nearly as long as the Fothergills' lineage. I see nothing ahead that—"

"Alfred apparently overheard something, Elizabeth."

She was offended by his reticence.

"Please give me some credit for a bit more courage than your manner suggests," she stated, her eyes widening.

"It is far more ghastly than any one of us could have conceived."

She saw that his face had lost some of its normal rather ruddy color.

"Come to the point, Cyril."

"Two members of a Muslim terrorist group, or so it seems. Not that that is surprising these days."

Elizabeth's pragmatic side surfaced.

"How could dear Alfred, alarmist that he has always been, have heard anything at all if they were careful about how loudly they talked? Would they be so sloppy in this regard? Think of that, will you?"

"It is strange, I admit, but I have no idea what goes on in the minds of terrorists."

"Terrorists? Here? In England?" Elizabeth was shocked. "I must have been a thousand miles away to have missed what you were getting at."

"Yes, Elizabeth, but it goes deeper apparently, if Alfred is correct."

"Deeper than terrorism? Is there anything more unsettling than that?"

"Yes, dear wife, there is."

He frowned, wanting to please her but also feeling the need to be keenly aware of his wife's physical state. He could sense her health declining, though he had no documented medical reason to be concerned.

"They have targeted England, yes, but not only our country. They are going to go after all of Europe."

"And the Americans? I hope they will escape calamity yet again."

"Do not be so certain about that. According to Alfred, they want to destroy all of western civilization and remake it into an Islamic state."

That answer could not have been further from her mind.

"The idle words of godless men have left you in this state?" she asked, amazed, shaking her head in disbelief.

"Besides, how do you *really* know that Alfred Hatterley has reported accurately what those men supposedly said? He may have been reading more into their conversation than you or I would have."

Cyril admitted that that could be a possibility but he thought it a remote one.

"You do not know what he heard, no idle chatter this," he said. "Wait until you do, and then give me your reaction. Remember this: I would never feel as I do if it were only trivialities."

His expression chilled her, and Elizabeth knew that her husband's behavior was based upon something less bizarre and, therefore, less questionable than she had thought at first blush.

"Tell me, then," she persisted, "what exactly was it that these would-be terrorists were discussing?"

Cyril hesitated a moment. "Revenge for the losses their kind incurred during the Crusades, Elizabeth."

"Six hundred years later, they still want revenge?"

"Sixty years later, the Jews are no less concerned about what happened during the Holocaust. When a race of people is assaulted so grievously, how can they *ever* forget, even generations afterward?"

Elizabeth was shaken but also more sympathetic to what her husband was going through.

"Revenge so catastrophic as to make the rest of history's great tragedies seem the stuff of mere nursery tales for impressionable little children," Cyril continued. "In some respects, this obsession is behind 80 percent of what they think and do."

"After all these centuries, they still feel that way? Isn't that strange, Cyril, even in today's world of revenge-driven groups?"

What he hadn't told her was how they intended to accomplish their goals, and she asked him about this. Still reluctant to engage in conversation that he felt would upset her, Cyril simply looked at Elizabeth without saying anything.

"By an invasion?" she persisted. "Is that it, Cyril? Accomplishing now what they were thwarted from doing so long ago?"

"Oh, yes, that. . . ."

"I ask you again, my beloved, how?" Her anxiety was clearly building.

"Disease," he said as he exhaled audibly.

Elizabeth blinked several times. "I do not understand."

"From what I was told by Hatterley, whom neither you nor I has ever considered to be a devious or capricious sort of man, it is supposed to commence somewhere in Italy, and then be allowed to spread, Elizabeth, throughout the whole of Europe.

"To save ourselves, we would be forced to make a complex and ultimately unmanageable fortress out of Britain, preventing some good people from entering or leaving. But with so much coastline, we could never be entirely successful, you know. Some intruders would undoubtedly slip on through. And then the tumult would begin."

"It sounds like—" she started to speak.

Cyril could anticipate what she was going to say.

"Plague. . .yes, it does," he said. "And that may be exactly what they have in mind."

She was trembling now.

"Should you not tell someone in authority?"

"Alfred tried that. He told me that he went straight to Edling but he was laughed at."

One of Prime Minister Harold Edling's least endearing traits was a blatantly supercilious approach to much of life, making him not one of England's most affectionately regarded political figures.

"Surely you must realize that Lord Hatterley is not as well regarded as you are, my love," Elizabeth snorted. "Few lords are. Words of gravity from *your* mouth have far more weight."

Cyril smiled at the compliment.

"But it could be as you mentioned, just hearsay."

He blinked a couple of times as he spoke, wishing he had not done so, and hoping that Elizabeth would not pick up on this.

"Have you told me everything Alfred mentioned?" she demanded.

"I have."

"But you were in your study for a very long time, it seems. Surely you—"

Her mouth dropped open as she saw him wince.

"You went ahead and checked your sources over the Internet, didn't you?" she asked, pinning him down.

"That is what took us so long, Elizabeth," he finally acknowledged.

"What did you find out?"

"There is *something* going on, something definitely simmering out there."

"Which could hardly have been started by what was overheard in a conversation between two Muslims."

"Right, Elizabeth. Here's another detail, what Alfred told me about their ages."

She waited for the next bombshell.

"Both were quite young apparently. If they were Irish, you could picture them in some news footage throwing Molotov cocktails at the British in northern Ireland. Astonishingly young, he thought, not more than teenagers!"

"I wonder. . ." she mused.

Elizabeth's thoughts drifted to a ministry of sorts that she had started during the previous decade, working with young people whom the government thought had potential to change their lives, steering them away from a variety of crimes.

"About what, dearest?" he asked.

"Nothing, I guess. Just a strange thought."

"Now it's your turn to come clean!" Cyril chided her.

"I have noticed something over the past two or three years."

"About the teenagers you have in here once a month?"

"Exactly them, Cyril."

"What have you noticed?"

"A growing bitterness."

"The ones who have suffered some form of abuse at the hands of their parents or siblings?" Cyril guessed.

"Certainly *they* are at the center of it. But it isn't just with them, for they have been bitter for some time, and with good reason. I guess it goes beyond bitterness *per se*. They feel so hopeless, thinking that their circumstances will never improve."

"With you there to encourage them, to build them up, and yet they still give you that impression, I must say that they sound like the ultimate hard cases."

"They may be just that."

"Has religion failed?" he asked.

"Mightily, I am afraid. So many churches are given over to show business Christianity. This is more apparent in the United States, I suppose, but it is coming to be the case in England as well. The emptiness of it, the falseness of all that glitter, those plaster smiles, these kids find it repellent."

"Any danger connected with them?"

"Yes, there is, Cyril. I wonder when the first one will find a gun and murder thirty children in a schoolyard. The others could start thinking that, at least, the bugger is *doing* something that the establishment will notice, and be forced to respond to rather quickly."

"By murder?"

"So many feel that they are the ones who face death at the hands of an incestuous father, an abusive older brother, a—"

She looked at Cyril with a sudden expression of fear.

"Society itself. Some have entertained the notion of killing the offending family member."

"And the others? The ones that feel society in general is to blame?"

"The worst cases have stopped coming recently."

She stopped, thinking how peculiar that was.

"They seemed, at the start, the most eager since they were the most desperately in need of the right kind of fellowship."

"Why did they stop? Was it as a group, Elizabeth?"

"It was. And I don't have a clue as to what is going on with them."

They lapsed into silence, holding one another.

It was Elizabeth who started speaking again.

"So, do we sit back and wait?" she asked. "Is that all you and I and others have left, Cyril?"

"Or launch another crusade of sorts," he said darkly. "It

is not difficult imagining, once the facts become well-known, air raids against the suspected strongholds."

"After the plague germs have been spread to every corner of the earth!"

Cyril's teeth were chattering.

"Foreign battlefields soaked in the blood of our brave men," Cyril said sadly. "How many more times must this happen, Elizabeth, how many more?"

"Or allow plague to wipe out entire villages," she added. "It is a choice over which the devil must be rejoicing."

"Or both, Elizabeth," he remarked, shivering. "It might be both, you know. While we are fighting the terrorists thousands of miles from here, it could be that this insidious plague has already started in some village and isolated hamlet—"

Cyril did not have to utter that last word for Elizabeth knew what it was and had begun trembling as well, her body suddenly chilled.

"Hold me, my love," she muttered, rampant visions of rotting, maggot-filled corpses mocking her as she tried to shut them out.

And this he did, needing Elizabeth's familiar warmth just then as much as she was craving his own. They briefly stood like that, remaining on their feet, bodies pressed close to one another, until a servant of many years' standing took the liberty of checking in on them because of concern over the lateness of the hour.

"May I prepare your beds now?" he asked.

"Yes, we will be leaving my study shortly," Cyril told him, slightly embarrassed.

After he was gone, shutting the door behind him at Cyril's request, Elizabeth asked, "Could they really do this? The distances are so great, the uncertainties overwhelming."

"I have been thinking about that," he allowed with some weariness. "What might the Muslims be expected to do? They would have to manifest an extraordinarily meticulous organization, timing, all the rest. Transporting canisters of germs to key population centers and—"

"Would it have to be so obvious?" she interrupted. "Couldn't germs be carried another way?"

"In something as simple as test tubes, Elizabeth!" he exclaimed, snapping his fingers. "In flat rough culture containers sewn into the lining of a coat, for example, undetectable, I am sure."

He lowered his voice, not out of secrecy but dejection.

"The more civilized we have become in this country, the more complex everything seems to be. The enemy does not have this Achilles' heel. They can think in simplistic terms. First, they decide that they want to destroy us. Second, they find a way to do that. They have no political, moral, or ethical obstacles to slow them down. They have no other mission but this one!"

His face was white from the impact of what he had reasoned out for himself.

"They would require just a few hundred glass or plastic containers."

"Not even that, Cyril," she said.

He was not sure that he wanted to hear the rest of what had occurred to her.

"Plastic sandwich bags, at least something that has the look and feel of those convenient little buggers but tougher, airtight, no germs getting out until the bags are opened."

Elizabeth drew on her experience doing volunteer work at St. John's Hospital in central London.

"The hospital was experimenting with these and I think the bags were generally considered as good as any of the other containers and less expensive.

"How could detection devices deal with *those,* Cyril?" she posed, hardly able to swallow. "They seem no different from the kind in countless homes these days."

"The germs could be placed on substances that looked like ketchup, mustard, mayonnaise!"

At that almost whimsical revelation, their energies gave out. Finally making their way to the master bedroom, husband and wife managed a kiss good night, despite the disturbing news that had been passed along by Lord Alfred Hatterley. A welcome and refreshing sleep would become ever more rare in the coming days.

CHAPTER 3

He decided that he had to approach the prime minister without fail, as planned, even though he had no real hope that this would do any good. . . .

Cyril Fothergill waited briefly in a room reserved for the most important visitors, while Tory Prime Minister Harold Edling finished a transatlantic conversation with the president of the United States. Finally, the most conservative political leader since Margaret Thatcher personally opened the door to his inner office and said, "Cyril, Cyril, we must visit more often. Please come in."

Edling was physically the shortest European male leader since Napoleon Bonaparte, and Cyril towered over him, but politically and intellectually, he was considered a force to be reckoned with. A product of the computer generation, as could be seen by the two CPUs on his desk, Edling was observed continuously exploring the capabilities of the Internet.

"Amazing, isn't it?" Edling remarked as he saw his visitor looking at the equipment. "When kings ruled this nation, they had to depend upon horses, runners, carrier pigeons, and I cannot imagine what else."

After they were inside the office, an aide shutting the door behind them, the prime minister sat down behind his desk. "I can send messages via the World Wide Web to the leaders of a dozen countries in the course of just a minute or two. Amazingly, I can do all this for just a bit over ten pounds monthly."

Cyril nodded, expressing appreciation for the technology. "Mr. Prime Minister, I am here to talk about something that may signal the dark side of the Internet."

"So you hinted during our conversation," Edling replied. "Please, sit down. I am hardly ignorant of the nature of what you mean to tell me."

He smiled pleasantly.

"You must understand that I regard you very highly, Cyril," Edling continued. "You should never make the mistake of thinking that I want your company only for, shall we say, purely administrative reasons."

Cyril thanked him for saying what he did.

"We all fall into behavioral traps, Mr. Prime Minister," he said. "I do apologize, for. . .I—"

"Forgive me for interrupting, but I think you could call me Harold and not risk a sentence at the bloody Tower."

Cyril smiled as he accepted the other man's courtesy.

"I am grateful for this privilege."

"Not all men have it," Edling reminded him.

Cyril sucked in his breath.

"What I must tell you, Harold, is very difficult," he said solemnly, though not in an exaggerated fashion. "I do not utter with any ease the words that bring me to stand before you this day."

A slight grin edged up the sides of the leader's mouth.

"Apparently so," he observed. "You seem to me now as white as a sheet."

"Something soon might be brought upon this nation and the continent beyond it and the world itself that is more serious than all the wars fought to date and any that might come to pass centuries from now."

Edling stood and walked over to a window that looked out over a rolling plain dotted with flowers that seemed to reflect the afternoon sun.

"Those are the most dire-sounding words you have ever uttered in my presence," he acknowledged, "and I know you well enough not to brand you an alarmist. I do trust you will justify yourself."

"I surely will, Harold," Cyril said, clearing his throat. "A band of terrorists may have a plan so evil that they can only be acting on their own. Not even the fundamentalist Muslim leadership would sanction anything as diabolical as this."

"Their kind always has a plan," Edling stated, chuckling ironically. "Was it not their original intention of invading Europe 800 years ago, that started the much maligned Crusades?"

It was no surprise to Cyril where the prime minister stood on that score, a conservative from birth, it seemed.

"If you had been the reigning monarch at the time, what sane man could doubt that the outcome surely would have been quite different?" Cyril said, partly to please Edling, but also because he honestly believed this to be true.

"Less bloodthirsty certainly," Edling agreed. "To thwart an invasion by any means necessary is one thing. That made sense then, and it still does. What alternative was there? Allow the Musselmen, as they were called, to slaughter those they deemed infidels from the Atlantic to the Mediterranean? Place a Christian Europe on the bloody altar of heathenism? Certainly not!"

Edling was showing more genuine emotion than usual, shedding the proper and reserved manner for which he was known.

"But I could not have sanctioned stopping Satan's evil barbarians with behavior that became grotesquely barbaric in itself," he went on, his cheeks bulging. "Killing the perpetrators in battle was required, and noble, and consistent with the original Christian mission. But slaughtering their children and raping their women?"

The prime minister of England shook with disgust.

"I can reveal my true feelings to so few people. You, Lord Fothergill, are one of them. That is quite a privilege and a trust, you know."

Cyril was honored and pleased.

"Now," Edling said, "what is the gist of this quite awful news? So far, what you have told me can be gleaned from the Internet on virtually any day, the ravings of a lunatic not part of any group. Surely that is not your source, I assume."

"It is not," Cyril assured him.

"I am relieved, and must ask you to accept my apology for thinking you as gullible as that. I did not listen to as much of Lord Hatterley's story as you, so I know a bit but not everything that you do, apparently."

"An attack, Harold," declared Cyril.

"An attack?" Edling repeated, jerking his head around. "Surely they know that they risk nuclear annihilation if we secure even so much as a hint that this is their intent."

"No, not by an attack, at least as you infer."

The prime minister was becoming more and more intrigued while trying to appear detached.

"Then by what means?" he demanded. "If we can rule out bombs and bombers and massive human waves, what is left? Or have I missed something?"

Cyril thought that the prime minister was beginning to mock him.

"I assure you that I am serious," he said, "and that I do not come here with any sort of cavalier attitude about—"

"How could I react otherwise, my dear Cyril? An invasion in itself does not stretch credulity, and I would have had our forces at the ready in less than a fortnight if I could have accepted what Lord Hatterley and you tell me. Do I understand that it is to happen not at first on battlefields drenched with blood, but rather, it is to come through disease? Is this your wild assertion?"

"Yes, Harold. I know that bombs and the like, placed in airplanes and shopping centers and government buildings and a vast array of other places, have been par for the course over the years. But then we have developed equipment and techniques that make detection less uncertain, and it is far more likely that terrorists can be caught as a result."

"Yet, suddenly, they change all this, you are saying, they are going a different route, instead of inventing explosives that thwart all our devices? Are they as cunning as you give them credit?"

"I do not know as much of history as you, but if I remember correctly, did not the First Crusade's leaders on our side of battle send some of their most efficient spies to poison the enemy's food and their water just as the offensive was beginning? Before we ever battled them *en masse?*"

Cyril was talking so fast that he was actually becoming out of breath and began to slow down.

"If your predecessors had had the ability to use *disease* as a weapon, can we say for sure that they would have hesitated? Could you picture Richard the Lionhearted pausing for an instant before embarking upon *whatever* course it took to stop the Musselmen in their tracks?"

Edling grimaced at a truth he knew all too well.

"But how could they achieve this? After all, Cyril, we are talking about an epidemic, not just a village or two being wiped out as a warning perhaps, imitating Hussein when he showed what he was capable of doing with *chemical* weaponry."

"First one canister, then another," Cyril pointed out with chilling impact, "then one sandwich bag, followed by many more in hundreds if not thousands of locations."

"Germs placed in *sandwich* bags? Did I hear correctly?"

"You did, Harold, you did. Put bacteria and such on substances that look like mustard or ketchup or even mayonnaise," Cyril said, remembering what Elizabeth and he had discussed. "How many schoolchildren could be wiped out in this manner?"

Edling nodded slightly.

"Cyril?" he spoke.

"Yes, Harold?"

"You mention children. Have you been aware of some talk lately, I mean, through the Internet and otherwise, about abused children fighting back?"

"Fighting back, through the courts?"

"I *assume* that that is it. Yet I do not know that I am convinced enough to *believe* it is, period."

"Getting back to our main subject, Harold?"

Edling shook his head vigorously as though to clear his mental cobwebs.

"Proceed," he said.

"Disease triumphs in an environment of filth. That may sound obvious but it deserves renewed emphasis. Even today, there are people living in filth all over Europe, especially in certain regions of Italy. I have never suspected the Italians of being champions of cleanliness!

"But also right here on the isles of Great Britain. London has its share of the worst poverty. I can drive just a few miles in any direction and show you where disease of nearly every kind could have a fertile ground. The poor often do not have even minimally proper housing, or clothes or anything else that is handed to you and to me every day of our lives until we are buried in graves or crypts or our ashes scattered to the winds. They do not eat as you and I the nourishing food that is our blessing. They exist on scraps. They often sleep in their own excrement. They—"

Edling was clearly affected as he took out a handkerchief and wiped his eyes.

"It is all that you say, Cyril," he said, "all that you say and worse. I was going into London last week. My limousine had to be stopped because of a body in the middle of the road. I thought he was just a poor beggar who had passed out. The man was dead, Cyril, he had been dead for hours, flies all over his body."

The anguish that Edling was feeling made Cyril even more sympathetic than he ordinarily would have been toward the man.

"Then something has to be done if there is the slightest possibility of plague as a weapon of war," he told the prime minister. "I would like to help. The man you saw presumably died of starvation. Think of the consequences of a plague, Harold, with tens of thousands of bodies piled high, perhaps hundreds of thousands, so many that our resources are taxed and collapsed, and no more bodies can be moved."

Edling nodded vigorously, relieved that he could count on support from someone who did not have intentions that were hostile, politically speaking.

"I will need it, this help you offer," he agreed. "I will need it desperately."

"Will you contact Adolfo?" asked Cyril, raising that subject for the first time. "He is a key to the success of whatever we attempt, as Clement VI was in the mid 1340s."

Pope Adolfo I was a man of the age, the first modern holy father to become captivated by the power of PCs. He was supposed to have a room in the Vatican that was filled with every computer-oriented device imaginable: wireless keyboards, laser printers, fiber optic network, and computers themselves that hit 200 megahertz of power.

"This pope is one of the most important keys you could imagine, my dear man. Protestants such as you and I have no equivalent, of course. If Adolfo can get hundreds of millions of Catholics stirred up around the world, then we can accomplish something remarkable, stopping the terrorists before they start. The new secretary general of the United Nations is a devout Catholic. So is the head of the World Bank, and, interestingly, the chap who presides over IMF [International Monetary Fund]. Innumerable ambassadors and other diplomats are as well."

Edling cleared his throat then continued. "I see no way around Pope Adolfo. He must be made aware of what could happen. It is Italy, after all, that would be hit first if you and I perceive the terrorists' master plan correctly. And he has excellent sources of information, I hear. Who is better at ferreting out details than a Catholic ordered to do so by the pope?"

"Do you think that this monstrous business can be stopped, Harold?" Cyril probed, while suspecting the answer.

"It is not so much whether it can be," Edling replied, "but that it must be, agreed? Assuming the information is correct in the first place."

Cyril had taken an expandable attaché case with him.

"Harold, may I put something on your desk?" he asked.

"Only if it isn't the results of the latest Reuters public opinion poll!"

Even Cyril found that amusing as he pulled a several-inch-thick computer printout stack of sheets and placed it before the prime minister who was sitting down now.

Edling flipped through sheet after sheet, periodically reverting to a stream of Latin phrases that Cyril understood to be dealing mostly with the dark side of human nature.

"The mad stand at the gates of hell, waiting," he said as he finished and put the pile to one side.

As he spoke, one hand reached out and impulsively gripped the other to prevent both from shaking.

"I live in fear," Edling confessed, with such chilling solemnity that Cyril felt some of his pain.

"Fear of what, Harold?"

"Fear of descending into madness. . . ."

"Are you taking—?" Cyril asked.

"Medication? I am, though, astonishingly, no one on the outside knows, not even the tabloids!"

Neither man spoke immediately after that, the fear of impending madness pervasive among kings and queens and emperors for generations consuming their thoughts. "Caligula. . . ," Edling said finally. "Nero. . .how many more? Even Benjamin Disraeli was supposed to have a problem."

"We may not be aware of the entire list," Cyril suggested.

"Was madness controlling them *before* assuming the throne or was it power that drove them over the brink?"

"Julius Caesar, the mightiest of the Roman emperors, once said that he envied those who did not occupy his position."

"His power turned his few friends into cowards and his many enemies into vengeful plotters," Edling reminded him.

Edling smiled ever so slightly.

"Are you surprised?" he asked.

"That you are learned about such matters?"

"Yes. . . ."

"Nothing about your intellect comes as a surprise. You have never found yourself deprived of an education equaled only by royalty."

"*Touché*," the prime minister replied. "But then there are some in this nation of sometimes effete snobs who think me barely competent, and covet the seat of power upon which I have been sitting."

Cyril shook himself in a gesture of disdain. "I am not one of their kind, Harold, you surely know that. I have never been among that group. Nor could I ever be!"

Edling glanced sideways at Cyril, more than a little amused that the other man's mouth had dropped open.

"So *serious!*" he exclaimed. "I fear only those unseen germs sent forth by heathen, not flesh and blood bodies that I can control with a snap of my fingers!"

Edling stared straight at his visitor this time.

"You will not tell anyone about my manner this day, will you? To the people, I must seem more stern, strong, someone with no weakness such as I have shown to you, either fear or careless jesting."

"Only the Heavenly Father Himself could pry a single word from my lips," Cyril assured the prime minister with great sincerity.

Edling reached out awkwardly and shook Cyril's much larger hand, then embraced him.

"And I, for one," Cyril whispered, "have seen more the strength of a man willing to admit his weaknesses."

Without warning, Edling asked, at barely more than a whisper, "Would you be the brave soul who agrees to leave for the Vatican a mere two days from now, representing his prime minister and the people of these beloved isles?"

Cyril knew that some kind of last-minute surprise from

the man was never less than likely, given the style of this particular head of government. Even so, he was nonplussed.

"I am not so eloquent as you may think, Harold," he spoke honestly. "Others are more gifted."

"They can speak words, yes, with greater drama, I suppose, but none has your heart, Cyril, none has your honesty. You would not be simply an actor repeating well-rehearsed lines but a man with a mission in which he believes mind, body, and soul."

Harold had him, and Cyril knew this, deciding not to risk protesting vigorously.

"Then I shall accept," Cyril agreed somberly. "What details must I know?"

"I will send with you one of my most trusted advisors, a fine man named Geoffrey Cowlishaw. But I have one condition from which I will not retreat."

"What is that, Harold?"

"That you not jest with him about his name."

Cyril was frowning.

"Why in the world would I do that, Harold?" he inquired, having no idea what the prime minister was suggesting.

"Cowlishaw means 'wood grimy with coal dust.'"

"Is that especially amusing?" Cyril asked dumbly, as humorless as ever.

Edling needed some considerable degree of self-control to restrain himself from tittering.

"It is after you have met him."

Cyril shrugged and then said, "I know just a little about this man, Harold. I have no doubt that we will be in harmony and that I shall like him."

Edling turned away, his manner becoming more serious than before.

"But you have heard of the growing disarray within the Vatican, have you not?" he asked.

"I believe so but I know little more than that. When did this start?" Cyril asked.

"Soon after the appointment last year of Adolfo's now-powerful personal assistant," he advised, clearing his throat.

"I had not heard of this."

"But then you are not prime minister," Edling said with a hint of sarcasm. "To the outside world, the Vatican seems every bit as implacable as ever. And secular governments are supposed to be guilty of intrigue! But since a ratlike little man named Baldasarre Gervasio appeared on the papal scene, matters have worsened, and assumed an edge that seems—"

Edling hesitated for a few seconds, trying to find a word that was as precise as possible. He did not want any doubt left as to the meaning he intended. Finally, he snapped his fingers.

"Sinister. . ." he spoke. "Yes, that is it. No other description fits as aptly."

"I shall take your word for it."

"Surely you feel the same way."

Cyril shrugged his shoulders.

"I am not positive what I feel," he replied, while realizing how evasive that sounded.

Edling pointed to Cyril's hands.

"But why do they glisten with perspiration? I take that as an indication of unease like my own."

"I have never based every view throughout the course of my life on mere feelings," Cyril told him. "To guide your day-to-day existence on that basis only is to walk on a kind of quicksand."

Edling applauded him, and said, "But you obviously do not realize that I am hardly the only one who has become uneasy over this. I know that Geoffrey intends to bring you up to date."

The men hugged once again, quickly this time, before anyone could see them, and then parted company. Seconds later one of the prime ministers's aides appeared and guided the special guest down the hall to the flight of stairs at the end and then outside to the awaiting unmarked sedan.

Prime Minister Harold Edling stood in the doorway to

that most private of his inner rooms until Lord Cyril Fothergill was out of sight.

I bid you Godspeed and protection, dear man, he thought. *None of us knows what awaits you.*

Briefly he sat down before his computer monitors and began surfing the Internet.

That group of terrorists that got away with kidnapping thirty Salvadoran government officials, then murdering each one, now has a page on the Internet! he exclaimed to himself. *If that is any indication of where we are headed, I wonder if I want civilization as we know it to survive. . . .*

He felt driven to his knees before a small but colorful stained glass window, the pieces of which had been painstakingly fashioned in Venice and assembled in London by English craftsmen who were provided the original design, the shortest prime minister in England's history praying with some fervor, a single ray of afternoon sunlight touching his forehead as though coming from the very throne of Almighty God Himself.

CHAPTER 4

Cyril Fothergill faced the members of his family with the news of the mission he had accepted from the prime minister. As usual, they supported him though all three had misgivings, particularly Elizabeth. Yet none could restrain their sense of pride, agreeing that his self-control, which had caused him to seem cold and unyielding before those moments he spent at his father's deathbed, would serve him well during any difficulties that might await him in the midst of the journey ahead.

Every member of the Fothergill staff bid him farewell, quite a few with tears slipping down their cheeks.

"A brave man!" one woman said.

"If anyone can perform an important mission for England, Lord Cyril is the one!" a gardener remarked, though neither he nor anyone else on the staff knew the purpose of the trip on which Cyril was embarking.

Cyril could have gone in the company of armed guards, but that would have drawn more attention than he thought wise. He turned for a moment and glanced back at the dozens of figures standing directly outside the castle's main gate. Would he return to them in a coffin so soon after his father's passing?

Cyril would discover that Lord Geoffrey Cowlishaw was a product of his privileged class, yet not arrogant and snobbish. This was the part that surprised Cyril. The other man had all the ingredients that should have made him insufferable.

Tall, handsome, and quite rugged in his appearance, to a degree that not a few women would find irresistible, he possessed broad, flat lips, nearly hypnotic medium blue eyes that seemed a bit smaller than normal, with a slightly Asian shape, and a considerable head of thick black hair. Moreover, he was clean shaven in a country where beards, mustaches, and tiny goatees, often heavily waxed, were the current fashion.

Lord Geoffrey Cowlishaw was standing alone, military straight.

This chap makes me look as though I have poor posture, Cyril thought, as he self-consciously straightened himself in the backseat of the nondescript sedan.

Positioned to one side of Windsor's front gate, he managed to look like a flesh-colored statue, and not much less impassive.

Everything prim and proper, Cyril observed, *waiting for us to begin our mission.*

Bags packed, his mass of hair was perfectly groomed, though a slight breeze was attempting to ruffle it just a bit.

And no entourage. . . .

"Every politician had enemies," Edling had stated earlier to Cyril, "and innocent people have been known to pay the price for grievances not their own. I would not want that on my soul when Almighty God calls me before His judgment seat."

While Harold Edling had no particular reputation as a devout Christian, that was more a result of his awkwardness over confessing his faith than an examination of his heart. But with Cyril Fothergill, he seemed to feel comfortable dwelling on matters spiritual.

"Drawing attention to yourselves could prove quite deadly if the terrorists should get wind of what your mission is all about," the prime minister had told the two men in separate meetings. "You should take a fair amount of baggage, as much as you can handle certainly, but, most importantly, with sufficient room to hide guns, mace, knives, and whatever other weapons you might need. And make no mistake— you will need these. Secrecy can be maintained only so long. That is why I am sending you over the channel in an old fishing boat, the least likely transport imaginable."

"I was concerned over that myself," Cyril acknowledged. "What happens if word does get out? Are we going to be like lambs before our Islamic slaughterers, even with a scheme as well planned as this?"

"I have prepared a list of contacts if you should need help or protection along the way," Edling added. "These are very powerful individuals who could instantly command small armies if the occasion arose."

The very uttering of those words was enough to make Cyril and Geoffrey—during their separate meetings with the prime minister—pause and wonder if this were one mission they should refuse after all.

"And beyond the danger itself, requiring us to put our lives on the line, all this could be for nothing, you know," Geoffrey acknowledged, now seated beside Cyril in the sedan. A driver would take them as far as the coast at Southampton, south and slightly west of London, where they would quickly board a seagoing vessel—considered a less obvious target of scrutiny since speed was thought to be critical—scheduled to stop at that port before recrossing the English Channel. "Adolfo has seemed curiously obdurate for some time, but never more so than when he took on that new advisor."

Cyril rubbed his arm, feeling a strange chill from his elbow to his shoulder. He, too, had picked up a discomforting tidbit or two about the man.

"A little chap named Gervasio. . . ," he agreed, nodding his head. "From what I hear, to say that he is unpleasant of countenance and temperament would be an understatement!"

The eyes. . .dark, like portals looking on a deep abyss. If the eyes were mirrors of a man's soul—!

It seemed that no one who met Gervasio came away liking him. Indeed, more than a few felt intimidated because he knew how to capitalize upon his position within the Vatican hierarchy and this, added to how most people reacted to him personally, made him formidable.

"You are correct," replied Geoffrey, pausing for a moment

to collect his thoughts. While he had heard a number of reliable accounts worse than what Cyril inferred, he did not want to appear arrogant before the man whom Edling had insisted would be his traveling companion, the man around whom the entire trip had been built.

He simply added, "I have heard some alarming talk about this character, talk not easily ignored, pointing to the occult and numerous secret meetings with certain terrorists."

That was as far as he dared go, for the message would seem only as believable as the messenger, and they did not yet know each other well enough to assume the other's credibility without question.

You do not have much of an impression of me as yet, Geoffrey was thinking realistically. *When you do, you will not be easily inclined to disregard anything that I say!*

"Wait a minute, Geoffrey," Cyril inquired, unwilling to let the matter drop right there. "How could someone as resourceful as Pope Adolfo not become privy to something as obviously noteworthy as this? This man, after all, is supposed to be God's vicar here on earth; is that not what Catholics believe?"

"I have no doubt that it is."

"Surely, then, the procedures within the church at present are more than sufficient to bar anything like that from happening? After all, it would seem that every last one of the fathers walking the corridors of the Vatican should be very concerned about the wrong influences gaining a foothold, demonic or otherwise."

The distaste Geoffrey had for Gervasio was evident.

"I cannot be sure," he acknowledged without hesitating. "But if it is true, then I have to believe that repulsive little rat is behind it all, and is holding something unseemly over the dear pope's head.

"Whatever is going on at the Vatican, none of it can be even remotely good if this Gervasio is involved. I fear for the future of Catholicism, though I am not Catholic."

Cyril then asked the obvious question.

"Do you know Gervasio?"

Geoffrey answered without hesitation.

"No, but others in my acquaintance do. He seems to have taken over, and blinded Adolfo. Not that this should have proven to be a difficult task."

"That must mean Gervasio has rivals who are probably out for the man's hide," Cyril reasoned.

"I am sure you are correct. For once I hope their kind succeed in whatever maneuverings they may be attempting."

Geoffrey paused, choosing his words carefully, not wanting to turn his traveling companion against him so early on in the journey. And he had to hold to his convictions.

"I suppose that I have to say this: Whatever it takes to get Baldasarre Gervasio out of there is fine with me."

He winced at the possibilities, which included assassination.

"Politics to the rescue of religion?" scoffed Cyril.

"For that bunch, the dividing line between the two is scarcely a gaping chasm."

Cyril began to feel that Geoffrey Cowlishaw was going to prove a bit extreme in his views.

"Are those priests not men of God, ordained by Him?" Cyril asked.

"Yes, but which god?" Geoffrey countered simply but with some profundity. "The Lord God Jehovah of divinely inspired Scripture or some other one altogether, constructed in their own power-mad image and strictly for their convenience, in order to fool the masses, a facade of godliness but without the power of the Almighty?"

He shifted in the seat, anxious to explain himself a bit better.

"I cannot envision that their main concern is ever going to be the spiritual benefit of any who look to them for divine insights. And that, I suppose, could explain why a Baldasarre Gervasio has been able to get in there in the first place.

"If the men around Pope Adolfo were more dedicated, he might not have had a chance to infiltrate the church. The irony is that they detest the little devil as much as I."

"Forgive me," Geoffrey remarked, catching the skepticism mirrored on Cyril's face. "Edling said that you were a man uncommonly stable in his views and—"

"Not easily intimidated by others with whom I might have little sympathy?" Cyril interrupted.

"Precisely. That was why I was so outspoken a moment ago. I did not think you would mind or be offended."

Cyril nodded. "It has worked to my disadvantage on occasion, making me seem something less than human."

"But you must think me too cynical, I am sure."

Cyril himself had been respectfully critical of what had been happening within the Roman Catholic Church, but he would never have gone as far as Geoffrey Cowlishaw.

"I must admit that I was leaning somewhat in that direction, yes," he admitted to the other man. "I have not as yet decided to accept as accurate all that you say."

"You and I will find out for certain when we reach the Vatican, I suspect," Geoffrey replied without showing any emotion.

"I gather that you do admit the possibility for some error of judgment then?"

"I would be dishonest if I said or felt otherwise."

They lapsed into silence.

Cyril had not traveled in that vicinity for a number of years. All of his business was in the British Isles, not on the continent. In fact, his daughters knew the route better than he, though they always traveled during the day. But the prime minister had decided that the secret urgency of their mission required going by the cover of night this time. And the captain of the vessel docked and waiting for them was one of Edling's most reliable subjects, someone who had worked for the prime minister before.

"He will not know why you are going to the continent," the prime minister told them, "and he is being paid not to ask."

Cyril and Geoffrey were able to find without difficulty the boat that had been selected by the prime minister for it was the largest anchored in the harbor that night, an old-fashioned vessel obviously left over from another era. After admiring it from the pier, the two men climbed on board the conspicuous seventy-foot-long, flat-bedded vessel of Greek origin but British ownership that would take them across the English Channel.

The ship's design, stemming from that of a type of vessel that was well regarded as far back as the times of the early Christian church, made it extraordinarily stable under the worst of conditions, and especially resistant to being flipped over on its side by violent winds because of its broad beam down the middle.

The first mate, a polite and cheerful chap named Randall Kirksey, who seemed far younger than others typically given that position on seafaring vessels, showed them to their quarters, which were on a par with the captain's, better appointed than they had had reason to expect but just as small.

Everyone else slept on the bottom level.

"At least we're spared that!" Geoffrey semed especially concerned about the cleanliness of the cabin.

After disposing of the several brown leather bags that he had taken with him, Cyril left his cabin and walked slowly to the stern, enjoying the smell of the pungent, fish-laced air. Standing at the wooden railing, he looked back at the docks, which saw far less traffic at that time of night and seemed at that moment nearly deserted. After a moment, the ship started to pull away from the port, its massive sails turned into the wind.

Soon after that, Geoffrey walked up and stood beside

him. "Something pleasant with which to start our journey."

"What's that?" Cyril asked, feeling more depressed than he cared to admit.

"The captain has invited us to his cabin for a special dinner in about half an hour. I did not accept for the both of us but said that I had to discuss it with you and get back to him."

Geoffrey clearly wanted to avoid disappointing the captain.

"Since he doesn't know what our mission is, I doubt that we need worry about any likelihood that he will pry too deeply. I think he just hopes to spend time with quality people."

He chuckled at that bit of self-aggrandizement.

"How uncouth of me! That sounded considerably more arrogant than I did intend. But then I suppose you and I often give hint of our upbringing in the very way we talk and how we hold ourselves."

Geoffrey smiled as he added not unsympathetically, "Shouldn't we be hustling about now?"

"Yes, that would be fine," Cyril replied. "I'll be ready in a little while."

Just before going back downstairs again, Cyril turned and whispered good-bye to England, part of him wondering if he would return to its shores alive.

Captain Letchworth was easily the tallest man Cyril and Geoffrey had ever seen, with a broad set of shoulders raising up a frame not of skin and bones, but an amply muscled physique.

At six feet, five inches tall, give or take an inch, he is the perfect height for someone in his position, Geoffrey told himself. *Intimidating without ever having to open his mouth. All he has to do is stand and glower to impose his will.*

When they went down to Letchworth's quarters at the opposite end of the ship, both men had to fight betraying their mutual surprise, yet they doubted that they were successful.

None of the guards I have is as towering as you, Cyril thought. *What a target you would be on any battlefield!*

Letchworth had a long, narrow face to match, the deep lines on his forehead and around his eyes as well as long ago sustained scars and blotches on the cheeks and chin showing that he had been around the block more than once, as the expression went. But he was affable, except when he stood to greet them, bumping his head on the ceiling of his cabin.

"No matter how often I do that, I never seem to learn," Letchworth told them irritably as he reached out to shake their hands and indicated chairs at the opposite side of the small rectangular-shaped table. "This is, after all, my ship. I'm glad the crew doesn't see how stupid their captain is in some ways."

After they had exchanged greetings, Letchworth announced, "We'll be having shrimp sautéed in garlic tonight. I hope neither of you has an aversion to shellfish."

"Not I," Cyril remarked. "But I cannot vouch for my traveling companion here."

"You needn't worry about me, either, sir," Geoffrey added.

"No sirs tonight," Letchworth announced. "We can be on a first-name basis, if that is agreeable."

"Then what is yours, Captain?" Geoffrey asked. "You know ours. May I say that you seem reluctant to tell us?"

"My given name is so awful, so cruel an act by my parents, that I decided long ago to use only my last name."

"I can tell you one thing," Cyril said.

"And what is that?"

"That you were born and raised in Hertfordshire."

"You speak correctly," Letchworth replied. "How in the world is it that you know this?"

"A pastime of mine is studying names."

"Then you have heard of mine before now."

"No, but I am aware of a village called Letchworth in Hertfordshire, one of my favorite regions."

The captain burst out laughing.

"Man, you are good at this," he commented, showing an appreciation that went beyond mere conversational banter. "I might say, very good indeed. Or cool, as some of the younger ones say."

"And you must be good at what you do," Geoffrey interjected. "This is quite a vessel, a daunting responsibility for any man."

"It is a direct copy of one of the finer Roman seafaring ships. I was pleased when I was offered my present post."

"How long ago was that?" Cyril asked.

"Ten years now. I started when I was thirty-seven."

"Aren't there more modern vessels that you could command?" Geoffrey asked.

"I suppose so but, speaking candidly, I have been known to engage in some whale business, getting carcasses to people who want them for one reason or another. Modern ships are vastly more expensive than I can afford."

Letchworth's demeanor was so casual that the two other men relaxed immediately and continued with the rest of the meal, which included perfectly prepared candied sweet potatoes with raisins, cornmeal mush, and, for dessert, apple compote.

"This is remarkable," Cyril said as he finished, "really remarkable."

"For shipboard fare, you mean?" Letchworth posed.

"I would be happy to serve such food in my home."

Geoffrey muttered agreement as he ate the last slice of apple.

"How could you do this well in such a cramped environment?" Cyril asked, impressed.

"I insisted, before I took this commission, that my men eat properly, and not work themselves to death, though this life is scarcely an easy one," Letchworth replied. "There would be no negotiation whatsoever about this point, if the owners expected me to accept their offer.

"Every last one of the crew is being called upon to endure hardship in the course of virtually every journey, not unlike seamen have braved for centuries. They must maintain their strength. And they cannot be fed slop, as is done by many other captains whom I know all too well."

Letchworth then added, curiously, "I try to inspire my men by being an example in another way."

"The way you talk. . ." Cyril ventured.

"Indeed! You *are* a surprise."

"It hardly took a giant leap of intellect to guess that. You speak well."

"Thank you," Letchworth replied.

"And I think you are a highly moral man. That is a fine combination: morality and intelligence."

"I doubt that other captains care very much about such matters."

"You may be right," Cyril acknowledged.

The plates and other items were then cleared away by that same young crew member.

"The French make a great show of the so-called art of cooking, as with everything that they do, flaunting their supposed superiority in a way that turns my stomach, if you will pardon my candor," the captain said, "but I prefer what the Italians deliver."

Cyril and Geoffrey sat on more comfortable padded benches, and Letchworth had the table removed so that they could continue talking to one another.

"What brings the two of you on such a trip, might I ask?" the captain inquired. "Business interests, perhaps?"

"Something like that. . ." Cyril admitted evasively but with little haughtiness.

"Forgive my curiosity. You both are obviously fine gentlemen. It must take something terribly important to drag both of you across the channel, especially during a time of year when storms could hobble us at any moment."

"We will be visiting a number of people in several

different countries," Geoffrey put in. "Lord Fothergill makes such a journey far less than I. For him it is a special occasion. My investments take me to the continent every year or two."

"You are going at a bad time," Letchworth repeated, "and for reasons other than the weather I mentioned."

"What do you mean?" Cyril asked, his palms suddenly clammy.

"I have learned some things from Vatican sources that are more than a little discomforting."

"Give us an example," Geoffrey prompted.

"A tolerance of the bizarre."

"There is so much that is bizarre in this world anymore," Cyril pointed out. "Which category do you have in mind?"

"The use of the Internet by a club of pedophiles is, as we say, the tip of the iceberg."

"*What?*" Geoffrey exclaimed.

"You heard me correctly. The Vatican should be very concerned about all of this."

"How could these perverts ever be stopped?" Cyril reasoned. "EWITT is not in full operation as yet."

"Agreed, Lord Fothergill. But then that is the tragedy, isn't it?"

Letchworth rubbed his forehead with his thumbs.

"Migraine?" Cyril asked.

"Not that."

"What is it then?"

"Just thinking."

"About what in particular?"

"The young, the usually defenseless."

"They seem to be fair game these days, don't they?" Cyril said.

"Yes, that *is* what I was thinking," Letchworth went on. "Abort them, mow them down in a schoolyard, abuse them at home, sell them drugs, then let some pervert rip their virginity from them. And what does the rest of society do? Moan, wring their impotent hands, talk about tougher laws, chatter, chatter, chatter."

The captain's eyes were bloodshot.

"Protestant churches should be joining together with the Vatican to *do* something. Any priest guilty of child molestation should be defrocked *immediately*. Any priest who seduces a teenaged boy should be kicked out even if the sex is consensual. But there is more of an interest in politics, in sweeping all these 'matters' under the proverbial carpet and all the while children are being attacked, with no one protecting them."

"You seem to know a great deal about the Vatican," Geoffrey commented.

"I do, young man. You see, Adolfo is my half brother. I have one other who is fully my blood."

"Pope Adolfo is—?" Both Cyril and Geoffrey wondered why Edling had not prepared them for this revelation.

Timing was crucial, it seemed with Letchworth, and he was enjoying the look of astonishment on their faces.

"And you must be wondering why I have chosen to captain a boat, any boat," he said, chuckling, "rather than use Adolfo's influence to get something bigger and better for myself."

Their awkward silence was a loud enough answer.

"I have never desired to be swallowed up into the mindless maelstrom of Vatican politics. You see, I have succeeded in convincing myself that I achieve as much as God expects of me for the faith without all the intrigue Adolfo endures every day of his reign."

Half expecting some semiliterate, rough-edged sort of man, instead of the well-connected captain across from them, Cyril and Geoffrey began to wonder if he were a key aspect of the prime minister's overall strategy.

Chapter 5

Just past midnight an excited but apologetic voice succeeded in awakening the new passengers.

"The captain urgently requests that you come on deck," the voice conveyed through the closed doors and grogginess of dissipating sleep. "He regrets awakenin' you both but feels sure you'll understand why after you witness what's happenin'."

Whoever was speaking caught his breath, then added, "Captain Letchworth asks that you hurry!"

Grumbling to themselves, Cyril Fothergill and Geoffrey Cowlishaw were prepared to be angrily combative with Letchworth, but that changed when they reached the deck. Neither spoke a word when they saw what the captain was pointing at beyond the bow of the ship.

Two whales. A very large mother and her young one of little more than two months.

"So young!" the captain exclaimed, much like a child confronted with a sight that would have previously seemed beyond the full exercise of his imagination. "And yet look at what that little one is capable of doing already."

Cyril and Geoffrey were transfixed but, unlike Letchworth, speechless as they took in a sight that blessed few men in those days.

The moon was full overhead, providing the only light for what seemed like a serene and evocative ballet in which the two mammals were gracefully participating, the silver light making it appear nearly surreal, as though the pair were somehow linked with the humans on board the ship in a collective dream.

"I'm guessing that the mother weighs many tons," gasped Letchworth, "but see how she succeeds in lifting herself out of the channel as though she is a simple butterfly moving from flower to flower."

An exaggeration, yes, but an understandable one, thought Cyril.

"And the young whale follows beside her with no seeming effort," he added, his voice husky with awe.

Geoffrey finally broke his silence, though getting the words out was not easy, even for a man as articulate as he.

"And the baby sometimes seems to be leading, teaching the mother a new movement," he observed with awe akin to Letchworth's. "Yet consider how long it is before a human infant can take those first stumbling little steps."

Cyril did not join in with them at first. He could not do anything but gaze at the whales with an almost hypnotic raptness, touched by the transparent affection that tied the two creatures together, creatures which brought with them every day of their long lives the ancient heritage that carried their kind through the many centuries they had been swimming the oceans of the earth.

The marine ballet continued with little apparent effort under that clear night sky not quite midway across the English Channel. . . .

For hours it went like that. The whales did not seem to be tiring but this was hardly so with the crew members on the ship only a short distance from them. One by one, they returned to their quarters to grab whatever sleep they could manage.

Only Cyril Fothergill, Geoffrey Cowlishaw, and Captain Letchworth remained, unable to break away, even as they dozed off periodically while still leaning against the wooden railing.

"I think. . ." Cyril started to say, then stopped.

"Think what?" Geoffrey asked.

"Never mind."

"I would like to hear what you were about to say, my friend."

"A ridiculous notion! I'm convinced that you both would

laugh at me if I told you."

Letchworth was the first to disagree.

"That'd be impolite, sir," he reminded Cyril. "I have Edling's wrath hanging over my head, ready to swoop down, remember?"

"I promise that we shall not do as you say," Geoffrey remarked. "You have my word."

"And surely you know that you have mine," the captain told him.

"They are *aware* of us," Cyril said.

Geoffrey and the captain glanced at one another. Cyril caught this, and, disappointed, shook his head.

"I thought so," he said. "You are laughing, but to yourselves."

"No," Geoffrey assured him. "My friend, my friend, believe me, it's not so."

"Then what?"

"Captain Letchworth and I were thinking about these whales exactly as you have been doing apparently."

"That they know we're here?"

"And both are showing off for us," Geoffrey went on.

"But it's absurd, can't you see that?" Cyril protested. "That was how I felt when the idea hit me and it was so silly, so unreasonable, that I brushed it aside instantly. Animals surely *cannot* possess the resources that many people think they do."

Letchworth would not let that pass.

"But why this show?" he broke in. "Whales have their motions, and they do what they do but never for as long as these two have been continuing. Couldn't that tell us something, something the Creator wants us to know?"

"And what could they be getting out of it?" Cyril persisted eagerly.

"Our pleasure, sir," he said. "They somehow gain some small bit of pleasure from ours, like actors on a stage responding to the hearty applause of their audience by bowing before them and then coming back for an encore."

The notion was so ludicrous on its face that Cyril was prepared to reject it as absurdist nonsense unbecoming a man of Letchworth's obvious caliber and experience, but, strangely, it struck a chord as he considered it, despite his initial rather cynical reticence.

He paused before musing out loud, "It seems to me that the lot of us did clap more than once, you know."

"And we called out to mother and child our heartfelt appreciation," Letchworth reminded him. "We were shouting accolades every few minutes. They must have heard. If they understood, in some basic way, that might be an explanation, it really might."

Cyril's face was flushed from forehead to chin.

"Having heard, they did not understand the language but they grasped the emotions behind it!" he exclaimed with sudden acceptance. "Congratulations, Captain! That must be it. That must surely be it!"

"When you pet a cat or a dog, and speak warm words, they do not know what you are doing the first time, nor even the second, but they have become more receptive," Letchworth said. "Soon enough they decide they like it."

He rubbed his chin, his intellect alive with the implications.

"Later, they sort it all out in their minds, and realize, in their own way, what you have been doing and why you have been doing it. It's obviously a fair leap to say this, with what little we know, but everything does fit if you allow yourself to look at it all with that final piece in place."

Geoffrey, having only listened for the past several minutes, decided finally to contribute whatever he could. "A bonding process. Imagine that, gentlemen!"

He thought for a moment, then added, "What if it's greater than what binds human beings together? Think of what that means. Think of how certain laws and social customs would have to be changed and the new ones that would be needed."

"Dealing with animal cruelty; are you talking about that sort of thing?" Cyril asked.

"Now you are seeing what I see!" Geoffrey exclaimed, his eyes sparkling under the light of that full moon.

Cyril and Letchworth, however, seemed dubious.

"For humans, there's any manner of motives involved," he continued, "manipulative, selfish, even brutal at times."

The other two men nodded as both suddenly caught Geoffrey's vision and recognized the sense of what he was speaking.

"Regarding animals, we can suggest, with some reasonable degree of certainty, that there is only the power of instinct guiding all of them—anything else would amount to placing these creatures and others on a level of creation that Almighty God never intended, I believe—from the top level of intelligence to the bottom, which manifests itself as love given for love shown, tenderness for tenderness, protection for protection, though hardly under these word labels."

Geoffrey saw that the other men were following every word.

"This is why dogs seldom have to be taught to defend their beloved masters," he concluded. "They do this out of their ageless instinct, which has never wavered over the years, just as when hunger strikes and they are driven to satisfy it any way they can, or the need to propagate, for that matter."

. . .which has never wavered over the years.

"Can we say the same?" he asked. "I doubt that, if we are honest with ourselves, we will ever be able to answer yes."

"I myself like someone one day and, a few weeks later, get tired of them," he admitted ruefully. "Marriages fail or they do not, but when they end, it usually has something to do with boredom."

Letchworth pointed toward the whales.

"My men were the ones who gave up," he reminded Cyril and Geoffrey, "not from boredom certainly but from sheer tiredness. I cannot picture even ebbing strength affecting animals. Once they accept a human being, that individual is never deserted or tired of, for animals seem incapable of acting in any other way but with total commitment."

He wiped his eyes, pretending to remove some speck of dust.

"That may be a kink for certain members of the animal kingdom, you know. What if they go on until they drop, and are of no use to anyone?"

"Perhaps we should go to bed then," Cyril suggested. "A few hours sleep sounds pretty appealing now."

As they were walking away from the railing, all three men noticed that the whales had disappeared.

Finding it difficult to get more than a few hours of sleep before awakening, Cyril washed quickly and threw on some clothes before heading up the stairs to the deck.

As he approached the thick wooden railing, he was surprised to find that he was holding his breath, concerned about whether the mother whale and her baby had become bored and left them permanently. Perhaps they would reappear at some point over the next few hours, to "perform" once again for everyone on board, presumably out of the sheer joy of doing so, including hearing their applause.

Am I making too much of this, Lord? he prayed to himself. *Or are You preparing me, and perhaps Geoffrey and the captain, for something this day?*

Now only a foot or two away from the hull of the ship, he started walking toward it much more slowly, not knowing why.

Oh, Lord, he gasped. *There is something wrong. You are trying to help me gather the strength to face it.*

He would carry the memory of those whales through whatever years that God, in His infinite grace, chose to give him. It would be something to tell his grandchildren.

Cyril peered over the railing.

Those whales, mother and child. Following the ship as the wind carried it across the channel.

They were close. Very close. Less than three feet from the side.

"Why are you doing this?" he asked the pair, half expecting an answer. "What is—?"

"Oh, it isn't so unusual, Lord Fothergill." The now-familiar voice of Captain Letchworth interrupted him.

Cyril did not turn around as the other man approached slowly and took the spot next to him.

"I can think of a number of instances," the captain added.

"Like this?" Cyril asked skeptically. "Practically rubbing up against the side of your ship, like some thirty-ton feline?"

"Not unusual at all. You are more accustomed, I imagine, to those lurid tales of yesterday, of whales attacking vessels such as this one and others much smaller. Certainly that happens, but what you witness now is more typical."

"I just cannot believe what I am seeing. I ask myself why. . .why a creature like that would do what she is doing."

"I have done some research," Letchworth told him.

"Captain?" Cyril asked.

"Yes, sir?"

"That doesn't surprise me, you know. I have been studying you a bit."

"And what have you decided?"

"That you are quite learned. That you decided education was something that could never be taken away from you, a judgment the Jews decided upon centuries ago. Their land, yes, their money, even their loved ones, but not their education."

Letchworth appreciated that.

"But I must seem a bit unusual from what you had expected of a fishing boat captain?"

"Actually, yes. I thought you were going to be a rough-edged character."

"Guzzling booze, eating with his fingers, perhaps picking his nose in public, like some character out of Moby Dick?"

Cyril was becoming uncomfortable.

"I didn't mean any of this as seriously as you are taking it," he replied.

"Taking it seriously isn't the same as taking what you have said in personal offense. I am not offended."

Cyril was relieved.

"I admire you, Captain," he admitted.

"Why in the world would you?"

"You have a gift of getting along with people, any type, any class. I feel much more awkward around strangers than you."

"Strangers come and go in my work all the time. I'd better get used to them, wouldn't you say?"

The captain was smiling.

"Now it is my turn at confession," he said. "Will you listen at least a little?"

"Of course!"

"You are not what I expected either."

"How am I different?"

"Most men of old money are self-centered, arrogant, domineering. But not you. I find that fascinating."

"Have you met many other rich chaps?"

"Quite a few. Didn't much take to any of them. Because they owned a fair amount of property, they acted as though they owned the whole world, to tell you the truth."

Cyril thought that changing the subject would be a good idea at that point.

"That research you mentioned, about whales. Tell me about it, will you?"

"I talk with captains of many other ships, and with the librarians of those companies that own them, as well as other good men who once earned their living from the sea."

"What have they told you by and large?" Cyril asked.

"From what I've been able to discover, whales of various kinds are given over, as a rule, to playfulness, and these motions we witness now are one way they have of engaging in play."

To Cyril that sounded reasonable.

"This ship is one big toy to the mother, is that what you are saying?"

"Something like that," the captain agreed.

"What else have you learned?"

Letchworth shifted his position more out of nervousness than discomfort.

"It all becomes a bit more complicated frankly," he said.

"Rest assured that I will pay attention as long as necessary," Cyril commented.

"There have been cases when whales have saved ships from great calamity." Letchworth spoke slowly, knowing that anyone not accustomed to such an idea would find it nearly impossible to grasp. "They seem at times like huge guardian angels. The same can be said for porpoises."

"That is much harder to believe."

"Undoubtedly, sir."

"But your manner suggests that you do."

"I try never to limit the instruments that the good Lord uses in His attempts to communicate with us."

Cyril was prepared to launch into a brilliant theological discourse, drawing from his years of study and training by tutors and others, some of whom were clergymen. But the captain's simple wisdom stopped him before he could part his lips.

"I am open to debate, Lord Fothergill," Letchworth told him.

"Captain?"

"Yes, sir?"

"Was there some other result of your research? Or have I misunderstood?"

"Oh, yes, there was."

"Tell me a little, will you?"

Letchworth licked his lips as he acknowledged, "Lord Fothergill, I have to say that it goes further than the last little revelation."

Cyril chuckled good-naturedly.

"You can bet on me being a gentleman in my response," he promised cheerfully.

"I sense some small possibility that whales may be capable of foreboding," Letchworth said.

The captain assumed that that remark would stir some reaction, but he was surprised when Cyril's response proved to be more restrained than he had guessed.

"What you have said may sound bizarre but I hardly think of it as blasphemous."

"I am certainly glad of that, sir," Letchworth replied. "I imagine that you have been exposed to considerably greater biblical training than I."

He turned toward the whale which, together with her baby, was still swimming alongside the ship though at a somewhat greater distance than before.

"These creatures may have, some scholars believe, perhaps the largest brain of any animal," the captain stated. "And from that, one can reasonably fathom whales possess greater intelligence than even the finest dogs or cats."

Cyril was becoming nervous.

"Then you have to wonder about something else: Does greater mental ability carry with it an equivalent abundance of senses? Aren't we edging close to dangerous speculation if we consider anything like this?"

He frowned deeply as he added, "I am not sure, now, that I like where you are heading, Captain, unless my brashness causes me to misunderstand."

"Rest easy, Lord Fothergill," Letchworth said, carefully avoiding any hint of condescension. "I am not implying any crystal ball nonsense. Only God and His anointed prophets have shown any ability to know what the future is going to be like."

"You are being dogmatic."

"I suppose I am."

"Consider this: Cats have eyesight that permits them to see in the dark far better than human beings are able. They and dogs and innumerable other creatures have a much more heightened sense of smell. And so it goes, ability after ability."

"What are you saying, Captain?" Cyril asked, betraying a flash of impatience, but not wanting to irritate a man whom he had come to respect.

"I have no idea, to tell you the truth. But look at them, sir. . .is that what you would have expected from any creatures of the sea?"

The mother was not much shorter than the ship. She could have done it some damage if she had chosen to attack. But that was not what she wanted.

"There have been cases, to my knowledge, and I do know a great deal about the subject, when such a whale, perceiving a threat from a ship like this one, would attack it instead of what she is doing."

"Has every whale attacked every ship?" Cyril asked.

"No, sir, but then none of them, as far as I have heard, seems to have ever acted in the manner that we are seeing."

He held up one finger, a thought occurring to him, and by that motion silently asking for a moment to address it coherently.

"But dolphins have behaved similarly," he went on. "They seem to be inclined as a group of creatures to—"

Suddenly a sound was heard. Wailing, pitiable.

Even as the mother whale raised her head slightly out of the water and turned it toward them, her cry continued uninterrupted.

Letchworth uncharacteristically turned away and clamped his hands over his large-lobed ears.

"I can't look at her," he muttered. "I can't bear that sound . . .that desperate—"

It did seem inexpressibly sad, a sadness that even a man such as Letchworth could not endure for long. Still Cyril was fascinated at the intriguing cry, a sound unlike that from any creature with which he had come into contact.

Geoffrey had come up from his room below a moment before and was now at the railing.

"I could not sleep after I heard it," he confessed to the two men. "It seemed to pierce the thick wood of this sturdy vessel, a sound unlike anything else in my experience."

Geoffrey was not alone. The crew members were now awake and beginning to struggle up the steps from their own quarters. In a short while they all were pressed against the railing, leaning over for as good a view as they could manage.

And the mother seemed aware of them all. But this did little to satisfy her, for she continued that wailing at least another full minute or two, causing several of the men, veteran seafarers though they were, to turn away and try to block it out as Captain Letchworth continued to do.

When the mother ended the sound that troubled so many, she and the baby dived beneath the surface of the water.

The two were not seen until much later.

When mother and child finally did appear, they had surfaced some distance from the ship and were not spotted as easily as before.

"Jus' look at the two of them!" one of the two men aboveboard remarked. "I'm awonderin', you know, why they're so far away this time?"

Letchworth and his two passengers had just finished another fine dinner and were climbing the stairs to get some fresh air when they overheard the sailor's observation.

"What in the world are you doing up here?" Letchworth asked. "Aren't you having any dinner?"

"I wolfed down my food, sir," one of the men confessed. "The others aren't finished yet. They don't eat near as fast as I do."

As the man smiled, he showed uneven teeth and a scarred upper gum.

"They never had the 'perience I got, I guess," he added, "I mean, havin' their food snatched out of their mouth by someone who needed it even more badly."

He said that he was hoping to stay and get some extra time watching the two whales.

"Fine with me that you remain here with us," Letchworth told the man. "It is good to have your company, William."

"You mean that, sir?"

"I surely do."

The crewman was pleased, his face breaking out in a broad smile as he leaned against the railing and surveyed the water.

Letchworth turned to Cyril and Geoffrey.

"I have always disliked rushing through the eating of good food," the captain told them, "but the three of us will live to eat again, if you know what I mean. Only slow eating brings the appreciation that good cooking deserves."

"How much longer will we continue to see what we have been seeing? That is another matter, am I right, Captain?" Geoffrey smiled knowingly. "Isn't that at the heart of what you're saying?"

"You read my mind, Lord Cowlishaw!"

"No, Captain, just that very open spirit of yours."

"Shall we stay here then, gentlemen?" Letchworth asked.

Both nodded.

"Good!" he said.

At first they could not see the whales, despite William's energetic pointing. A heavy cloud cover that night made detecting anything in the channel most difficult.

A short while later, though, the mammals came closer to the ship and could be seen clearly as they started going through what had become a regular routine, a show that seemed to be choreographed just for that particular audience.

But there was something different about it this time.

"The mother seems to be trying to get the baby to balance itself on her back somehow," Letchworth observed.

"Yes. . ." Cyril agreed. "I see that!"

The mother whale would swim along, her body submerged except for the main fin on her back. Her young one at first stayed by her side, nearly below the surface of the water in a similar manner.

Then the mother would "duck" under the little one.

"Look at that!" someone shouted.

The mother came up, forcing the baby to surface, but it became confused and swam to one side.

Again and again. . . .

"The baby hardly seems so intelligent now," Geoffrey said, some sarcasm creeping into his voice.

"How smart were you at two months?" asked Cyril jokingly.

A fifth try, a sixth one.

The crew member was stretching his upper body over the railing, waving at the baby whale, telling it to pay attention, hoping the sound of his voice somehow would spur it on.

At the seventh attempt something wondrous occurred.

"At last!" Letchworth yelled. "At last!"

The little one realized what its mother wanted.

And rode on her back!

The four men on the deck gasped at the sight.

"Unbelievable!" one crew member exclaimed.

And that was what it seemed, a sight that perhaps no one else in the known world at the time had seen before then.

That one man was followed by his mates who began shouting whatever came to their minds, savoring what the baby had done as though it were their own triumph.

"But why?" Letchworth mused. "What possibly could be the mother's purpose in doing something like that?"

Suddenly his words seemed to choke in his throat.

"Captain?" Cyril asked, alarmed. "Are you—?"

He was pointing frantically.

"There!" he managed to say. "There! Oh, no! No!"

"What is it?" Geoffrey asked, alarmed by a shout of panic from a man as seasoned as this captain.

"Don't you see?"

"See what, Captain?" Geoffrey was confused.

"There! Even on this night it should not be at all hidden from your view."

He pointed north.

"To their left and, now. . .to the. . .the right!"

Cyril and Geoffrey suspected that it was hardly customary for Letchworth to act so flustered.

He seems almost in a panic, Cyril thought.

"Captain, I am sorry," Geoffrey said, "but I cannot—"

Suddenly he glimpsed the ominous intruding fins, first one, then another, then several more, coming in east and west of the whales.

"Sharks!" Cyril finally blurted before Geoffrey spoke again. "Sharks are heading toward those whales. But why? What could be attracting them? I have read that they sense only bodily fluids in the water such as blood."

"There must be a cut somewhere on the mother or the little one," Letchworth said, barely able to control himself. "It is not possible that there would be so many—" He seemed to choke again on his words.

Half a dozen fins were visible now. Then another, another, still another shark. After only a minute or two, an army of sharks was assembled, possessed as they were of some sense that drew them to meat that they could not possibly smell from such distances as they had come.

But the whales seemed to be ignoring the sharks, or strangely unaware for the moment, as they continued their mesmerizing movements. First out of the water, soaring through the air with such grace like bloated flying fish displaying breathtaking agility, then down again, the whales repeated the motion over and over, their high-pitched voices sounding like out of tune piped instruments without the rest of the orchestra joining in with them.

"Whales are naturally quite peaceful," Cyril commented. "They will not engage in a fight unless they are forced to do so."

"But the enemy's forces are growing," Letchworth reminded his passenger. "Soon the sharks will be a match for the mother, if only by their numbers."

"Still, Captain, they are nothing compared with her, mere pygmies, I tell you. . .nothing compared with a devoted mother protecting her newborn."

"Do not be too sure, Lord Fothergill."

The crew member with them swallowed a couple of times. He was hesitant to say anything that might irritate his captain, especially in front of strangers who were his guests, but more out of respect than fear of any kind of punishment.

"What is it?" the captain asked.

"Sir?"

"Speak up. You are distracting me."

"Sorry, sir. I am sure that my mates would like to join me, especially now."

Letchworth nodded, without facing the crewman.

"Tell them it is permissible to do this," he said, his voice showing a certain warmth amid its authoritarian sternness that seemed touching to Cyril and Geoffrey.

In seconds, the other members of the crew were climbing up the steps and rushing to the side of the ship, their gasps the only sounds apart from the relentless slapping of water against the hull and the splashing of the whales as they continued their midnight ballet, while sharks gathered some distance from the mammals.

Finally, the attack came, with a swiftness and a slashing, primitive brutality that stunned even the veteran seafaring men.

One shark at a time struck initially, distracting the mother, not getting close enough to tear at her huge body but starting the moment by moment process of wearing her down, a process that would take more than an hour.

This uncompromising spectacle would force captain, crew, and passengers to remain on deck, scarcely moving, their attention riveted on what was happening only a hundred yards off the side of the vessel.

The mother was able to dispose of the early attackers easily, knocking them to one side or another. But she also had to keep her largely defenseless baby in sight, and this distraction wearied her before long.

"Why doesn't she just swim off?" Geoffrey asked. "She seems to be acting stupidly now."

"The sharks would only follow right after her," Letchworth told him. "Nothing could be gained, and, in the meantime, she would be using up her energy even more quickly."

He shook his head.

"No, that mother must stand her ground, her water, if you will, and hope that these attackers give up the battle before her strength is completely gone."

That might have worked if there had been only a few sharks in the vicinity, for the mother whale was twenty times heavier than a single shark. But their numbers were being constantly replenished, two appearing to replace each that the mother annihilated.

"They are being attracted from miles away, from all directions," the captain added sadly. "She will cave in before the sharks go elsewhere."

Each shark came closer and closer as their numbers increased, forcing the mother whale to scatter her attention too incompletely among the growing horde. First one took a small piece out of her hide, then another followed, doing the same, and another, each coming away with at least a partial mouthful of meat. The spilling of her fluids drove the sharks to a heightened frenzy.

"Where is the young one?" Letchworth screamed out, embarrassed to show such emotion but unable to hold himself back.

"Over there, to the right, sir!" someone exclaimed in a shriek. "Two sharks are dragging the poor thing away, though it is struggling to get free!"

In a bizarre coincidence that gave every man on board that ship the impression, however fanciful, that she understood some sense of what had been said, the mother whale lumbered frantically toward the little one, her own massive weight dragged down by sharks hanging onto her as they tore into more and more of her body.

As though asserting momentary supremacy, she sank her massive jaws into one shark, then another, cutting in half both creatures.

And then she dived underwater.

"She's leaving the baby!" a crew member shouted.

"No! No! No!" rippled through the crew members.

But the mother whale had something else in mind, something she needed to do while still having life within her, something so extraordinary that every man on the deck of that ship, including its captain, Cyril Fothergill, and Geoffrey Cowlishaw, would go to his grave with the sight unforgotten.

The mother rose to the surface again. . .underneath the baby!

"Now we know what she was up to earlier, teaching her little one as she did!" Letchworth exclaimed.

"But what does that have to do with the sharks?" Geoffrey asked.

"I'm not sure as yet. I—"

At that moment the baby whale was being guided hurriedly toward the ship.

In less than a minute, mother and child were beside the vessel. Sharks trying to get in back of her were banged into the hull instead. The mother was able to stun at least one with her large tail and bite off the head of another.

"By simple good fortune or deliberate planning, she seems to have succeeded in limiting the directions from which the sharks can continue their attack," Letchworth said, aware that he might be judged guilty of ascribing to the animal more ability than warranted. "Now they are unable to get behind her."

"I think it is something else altogether, Captain," sensed Cyril. "I think we may be witnessing a surpassing display of something approaching pure love."

The sharks continued to ravage the large whale, chunks of meat scattered over the water's surface.

"How long can she stay that way?" Geoffrey asked. "There will be nothing left of the poor creature!"

And then everything the mother whale had done seemed insignificant and mundane when compared to her next and final act.

She pulled her body partway out of the water, the baby on top of her, their bodies barely touching.

Crew members gasped at the sight.

"She is giving her offspring to us," Letchworth stated, awestruck.

"That seems completely absurd, Captain," Geoffrey observed.

"It is not! May I say that you don't know everything, Lord Cowlishaw. That mother wants us to take care of her child, to protect it because she no longer can. Is she supposed to abandon it to the sharks?"

"It is not her devotion, Captain, that I doubt. It is how you imagine she will now manifest that devotion."

"With all respect, you're very wrong, sir!"

Raising his voice, he told the crew members what he thought. . ."That mother wants us to take care of her child, to protect it because she no longer can."

Deeply affected by what they were seeing, every man on that ship echoed their agreement. And all were ready to do whatever their captain asked of them.

"There is no time even to gather together the ropes!" Letchworth told them. "It is just too late, too—"

The mother seemed to be looking at him, studying him, her tiny eyes opening and closing in pain.

"We'll have to get the ropes around the baby and. . .and pull it up, we would—" The captain broke off in midsentence as he turned to face her. "You'll be gone by then, down the bellies of savage predators, and your child along with you."

Then she dived down. And the baby followed her.

"Stand back!" the captain bellowed to his ship's crew. "Clear the middle of the deck! Do it now, mates!"

"Is she going to throw—?" Cyril started to ask, his eyes shooting open as he guessed why the other man was responding in that manner.

"That is what I am thinking, yes," Letchworth replied in a much lower voice. "For the sake of these men, who must believe in their captain every step of the way during this journey and every other henceforth, you and Lord Cowlishaw must humor me for the moment, despite any contrary feelings you might have, and act as though I am quite sane, instead of suffering the delusions of too many years at sea, which would cause a loss of respect in their eyes."

He drew his lips tightly against his teeth.

. . .*respect in their eyes.*

"If I do not have that, I have nothing," the captain added, "perhaps less than nothing."

The mother whale broke the surface, the baby pushed directly above her, barely touching her back.

"She is going to—!" Cyril exclaimed.

With one mighty flinging motion of her upper body, she tossed that much smaller body but still bulky form through the air, as though it weighed little more than an ordinary dog or a cat instead of greater than a ton.

The baby whale hit the railing, cracking that section in half and then slammed against the deck with enough force to cause the ship to shudder from side to side, knocking every man, including the captain and passengers, off their feet.

The mother started emitting a plaintive cry until she had no strength left, and the baby whale answered that anguished call.

Everyone stumbled to their feet, rushed over to the side of the ship, and pulled back immediately, unable to endure the sight that met their eyes.

More than a dozen sharks were in a frenzy, ripping and pulling apart the mother's body like giant piranha displaced from the Amazon.

She was not quite dead but she could no longer resist, parts of her spine now visible along with other areas of bone and raw, red-tinged muscle.

"The whale pole!" Letchworth commanded. "And hurry!"

A crew member quickly retrieved this from the other end of the ship where it had been strapped, a seven-foot-long, thick wooden pole with a hooklike metal end edged by a series of jagged prongs, a weapon that was undoubtedly an early version of what had become known as a harpoon.

"Not every whale is friendly," the captain told Cyril and Geoffrey defensively.

He expertly grabbed the middle of the pole but hesitated as tears stung his eyes and poured down his long, thin cheeks.

Cyril touched the captain's shoulder.

"You must," he whispered. "In the name of mercy you must do this. Everyone is supporting you. There is no shame."

Letchworth shot him a withering look and Cyril stepped away.

As the captain glanced over his shoulder, he saw that all of the crew members had gone to their knees, praying, hands joined in an unbroken human chain.

"Merciful Father God," Letchworth said out loud, "lay this not to my charge, I beg You. I seek only that poor creature's freedom from pain I myself cannot bear even to imagine."

He estimated the distance and, waiting only a moment, threw the pole. The heavy weapon hit the mother whale through her right eye, bursting that tiny organ like a fragile soap bubble. Responding with sudden, mindless movement, her entire body shuddering, she leapt out of the water, raw gaping wounds visible to those men who forced themselves to watch from nearby, but then emitting no sound of any kind, she dropped back down a final time, her now lifeless, battered carcass soon sinking out of sight.

"The baby!" Cyril yelled. "Pay attention to the baby!"

Flopping its tail against the deck, the little whale started emitting a mewing sort of sound, apparently calling for the mother.

"Oh, Father God!" Geoffrey the cynic could not face the men and turned away, his back slumped, sobbing to himself.

Cyril saw Letchworth abruptly straighten himself and throw his shoulders back.

"Water. . ." he ordered. "From what I have gathered over the years, regarding those that have washed up on the beaches of Brittany and elsewhere, if she dries out, she dies. You must not delay in this! She must be kept wet!"

"She?" Cyril asked rather stupidly. "How can you possibly tell what that whale is?"

The captain did not answer, dealing with him as though he were an upstart student too naive for his own good. One of the crew members brought him a bucket of water almost immediately.

"No!" Letchworth stated firmly but without anger. "Seawater. Get ropes, all the buckets we have. Lower them over the side. Whales cannot live with the same water that we use."

He patted the man's right cheek.

"It is all right, Henry," he said, softening his tone. "I am not upset. Do step lively though, please, mate."

Relieved, Henry hurried on to the task he had been given by his captain, directing the others to do the same.

"He has never been 'right,' that one," Letchworth told Cyril.

"Do you know how he came to be that way?"

"I cannot be sure, Lord Fothergill. Henry is exceedingly gentle, obedient, good-natured, like a friendly mongrel dog which is out to please everyone in order to gain acceptance so that he will not have to walk the streets again."

"Was that where you found him?" asked Cyril.

"No. . . ."

"I am being too personal. Forgive me."

"Henry is my brother, sir. When he was young, he used to wander off, a child walking the cruel streets. We did not understand him in those days. In time, because we became more alert to his needs, he showed himself to be much happier, and made our lives easier in the bargain."

Cyril was surprised, of course, but he tried to avoid letting his feelings show.

"At first the crew members objected quite loudly when I brought him on board some few years ago," Letchworth continued. "You see, he is not capable of doing much of anything, and for us to survive on journeys much longer than this one, and to prosper. . . ." His voice trailed off but his meaning was clear.

Cyril saw how much a struggle it was for this man to keep himself financially sound.

I could lose all but a small percentage of what I have, he thought, *and still be quite well off for the rest of my life.*

He decided that when he returned to England he would approach Edling about helping Letchworth and his crew, perhaps with better wages or less rigorous routes.

"Henry is unable to navigate," the captain went on. "The whole idea of telling directions seems to confuse him. Nor does he participate in gutting any of the fish we must catch for food."

His tone softened and there was a slight smile on his face.

"My brother cannot bring himself to take a simple knife and slit their bodies open for the food they provide, even after each has stopped flopping around and is dead.

"Truly the gentlest man I have ever known," he said, obviously devoted to Henry, "without guile, anger, lust, or a great many other unpleasant traits common to the rest of us."

He sighed as he wiped his eyes.

"My brother there, my dim-witted, kindhearted brother, approaches a state of sinlessness though I know he will never achieve this fully until he reaches the gates of heaven and enters the kingdom."

Henry was the first of the crew members to return, not with one bucket of seawater but two. He splashed the contents of the first over the baby whale, then the second, refilling the buckets again and again, more frequently than any of the other men. It was at the end of the fourth trip to get seawater that he put the two buckets down on the deck and stood briefly in front of the little whale's snout.

"Why're you stoppin'?" one of his mates asked. "Aren't you helpin' the rest of us any longer?"

Henry smiled beneficently at the man but did not answer as he bent down, touching the whale between her tiny eyes.

"Sweet child. . ." he whispered. "Sweet lonely child. Your mother is gone, but she saved your life, and we are your family now, little helpless one."

He bent over, kissed her on the snout, and then stood again.

Crew members and captain alike were spellbound.

"He hardly speaks, my brother," Letchworth observed. "His sentences are often all jumbled up, hard to understand much of the time, but now this! He speaks foolishly but he speaks coherently! What is happening to him?"

He seemed to stagger, leaning against Cyril momentarily.

"Forgive me. . ." he said.

"I am not untouchable, Captain, but I am honored."

"You honored, Lord Fothergill? I appreciate your kind words but how can that be? I work with my hands, a lowly laborer compared to you. Why should you be honored?"

"You are a man I would be pleased to have living within my home, eating at my table, sleeping in one of my beds. I have no brothers. And I have felt some loss because of that over the forty-odd years of my life. I would have given up half my fortune in exchange, and I could have had no finer than you."

A moment later, the baby whale raised her head and opened her mouth wide.

"Henry—!" Letchworth shouted.

She seemed to be studying him. Then, suddenly, Henry hurried downstairs toward the galley area, leaving the buckets where he had put them.

The captain slapped his forehead.

"What a strange brother I have," he exclaimed without shame, "strange in more ways than one!"

While several crew members continued bringing buckets of seawater, the rest had little to do except their normal duties. Everyone stopped as soon as Henry returned to the deck, fascinated by what he was holding—one medium-sized fish in each hand.

He stood before the whale and held out a fish before the creature's nose. And she seemed to sniff it, interested, though hesitant at first.

Henry bent down in front of her.

"You mustn't do that!" Letchworth called out with great anxiety. "Whales can be dangerous!"

His brother turned briefly and glanced at him, but no fear was reflected in his eyes.

The whale was now opening its mouth, hesitation gone. Henry slipped one fish at a time into it, looking without any discernible nervousness at the sight of a full set of teeth ringing its gums. The first fish was swallowed with some difficulty but the second one went down much more easily.

"The whale must be very hungry," Letchworth said. "The rest of us might have been able to guess that sooner or later, I suppose, it is hardly a bizarre notion. But my brother seems to have known right away."

"Has your brother experienced any affinity for animals before this?" Cyril asked.

"Henry has always had a bond with them, from birds, cats, and dogs to lizards, snakes, and other creatures. They certainly have accepted him as he is, without regard for his hobbled brain. I believe, Lord Fothergill, that St. Francis would have been very pleased with my poor brother."

Once the whale was finished, Henry hurried back to the galley for additional handfuls.

"Interesting coincidence," Letchworth told Cyril.

"What is that, Captain?"

"We have caught more fish than we could ever need this trip. That is seldom the case. But it has happened this time."

Another voice intruded.

Geoffrey Cowlishaw had finally regained his composure.

"Sorry for that," he told them. "I'm not accustomed to feeling as I did when that mother made such a sacrifice. I've known no human beings who have acted in any way like that."

He shrugged his shoulders.

"The women I know are selfish, spoiled, unwilling to sacrifice their afternoon teas, let alone anything greater required of them."

"I would hope that you are not condemning all women?" asked Cyril suspiciously.

"Just the ones I have had anything to do with. There may be others. I hope many more are of a different temperament. It would be terribly sad if not."

"My dear wife, Elizabeth, is one of those, Geoffrey. She is like that whale, I am quite sure, willing to give her life if need be."

"That may be what you think, of course, and you are probably right. What do I know? But who can say what any of us are capable of until that moment of testing is upon us?

"Besides, look at me tonight, gentlemen," he continued, spreading out his arms. "I have fought in any number of places, almost to the environs of fiery hell itself, but a short while ago I could not bear an animal's cry of pain and—"

He paused, feeling rather foolish.

"Gentlemen, need my behavior this day be bruited about?" Geoffrey asked plaintively.

"None of it, Geoffrey, none of it," Cyril assured him.

"The same as far as I am concerned," Letchworth concurred. "Every man has such a moment. If he denied his emotions, I suspect some part of his humanity would fall by the wayside."

The baby whale, as yet unnamed by anyone on board, all eight and a half feet and nearly a ton of her, continued to flop around on the tongue and groove deck to such an extent that the crew was forced to tie her down as tightly as they dared, attaching a single thick rope around the section of her body just before her tail, with one tied to the railing on one side of the ship and the second to the reverse side. Another rope was looped around her head a few inches behind her eyes and secured as the first had been. They tried to get one under the middle of that young but already mostly unmanageable body, and failed.

There was little else that the men could do. They had no facilities whatever for routinely rescuing whales. Taking care of one in distress had never been a mission of theirs, either personally or for one of the companies chartering them, and anything they were able to devise was by its nature makeshift at best, even with someone as qualified as their captain guiding them.

"She does not struggle. . ." one crewman after another observed. "She seems comforted by what we are doing."

That veteran seaman was more on target than he knew. But what he did not realize, nor did anyone else on ship, was that she was simply waiting. Even if they could have guessed, they would not have known why.

"I know little about whales," Geoffrey said as he stood with Cyril and Letchworth, watching the crew do their best. "But many other creatures have been known to come to think of their human benefactors as a kind of substitute family. After a while, we are likely to seem rather like whales to that one."

"I know a man who certainly looks like one," Cyril joked, having in mind a lord from one of the northernmost estates, someone who did no work during an average day but spent most of his time eating imported food from the continent.

"So do I, come to think of it," Letchworth commented.

The baby whale was resting pretty well.

"Your men seem to have done it exactly right," Geoffrey said. "A remarkable group, Captain!"

"And the same ones, with a single exception or two, that I have been with for ten years now, and expect to have for at least that much longer," Letchworth said proudly. "I have come to know when those chaps are happy, when they are becoming ill, when they are nursing a grievance, you know."

He saw Geoffrey's dubious expression.

"I can tell all of this and more, sir, by watching carefully the way each of them walk, the way they hold their heads, the expressions on their unshaven faces, the tone of their voices, even how fast or slow they eat their food."

"Like a father. . ." Geoffrey suggested.

"Very much so, Lord Cowlishaw, you are right. Those men seem like my grown children. When we hit land, I am reluctant to see them go, even though my responsibility for what happens to them ends for the time being."

His voice then became softer. "When they have boarded this ship, though, it is my duty to protect every last one of them."

With the whale safe, all three men decided to go below and get some rest while the crew members went about their various duties.

Roughly an hour later a storm began to kick up. Letchworth ordered several crew members to stay with the sails and a navigator to steer the ship but the rest were ordered below.

"Stay at the ready just in case!" he exclaimed.

Henry, though, refused to leave.

"You must," the captain ordered. "Do you not understand that you could be swept overboard any minute?"

"I understand good enough," replied Henry. "But what if those ropes slip off the poor whale and she slides across deck and tumbles overboard? All our work for nothing then! And she dies as this storm rages!"

"I cannot take the chance, my brother, I love you too much. Surely you must understand that you are of greater worth than any animal to me and to the good Lord Himself."

Henry's eyes narrowed.

"Maybe it is that you love controlling me too much."

That hit Letchworth nearly as hard as a physical blow. What Henry said was so completely stark in its honesty, coming from someone he knew to be without deceit, that he stood motionless for a minute or two, the rain driving so hard against him by the wind that it stung his face.

"Forgive me," Letchworth begged as he hugged his brother. "Forgive me for ever seeming to do that."

"I never mind," Henry told him, raising his voice above the noise of the storm. "I know you want only to protect me. But I must do this for that poor creature. Right now, she is more defenseless than you think me to be."

"Then I will stay with you and help."

The intensity of the storm and the weight of the baby whale put a great strain on the ropes, which, now rain-soaked, started to slide down the rubbery surface of her skin.

"She moves!" Henry, flapping his arms up and down, shouted in near panic. "We need more rope. We—"

As the ship lurched suddenly, hit broadside by one large wave and immediately another, Henry was knocked off his feet.

"I am here with you!" Letchworth yelled to the other crewmen as he stumbled toward his brother. "Strap yourselves to your posts."

Those men had to remain on the deck because without crew members at the helm controlling the vulnerable sails, to whatever extent these could be, the ship was in great danger of hitting an unexpected obstacle, including a whale confused by the turbulence—stories of that happening were far from uncommon—or perhaps another seafaring vessel's wreckage, or turning too sharply, and aided by the wind, capsizing.

Henry had grabbed hold of one of the ropes around the whale, preventing him from being washed overboard. But the extra stress further weakened the tautness of the woven hemp material, the strands now softer and slippery with no friction to hold them together. The end tied to the railing started to slip. Henry noticed this and crawled to it, trying to pull it tighter and hold it back.

Cyril and Geoffrey's quarters were on the second level of the ship, the crew on the one below them. Awakened by shouts aboveboard, the two men dressed in heavy clothes which they had brought along since winter was approaching, with hoods over their heads, and rushed up the stairs.

They reached the deck just as Henry and the baby whale were tumbling overboard. Letchworth's scream cut through even the storm's noise as he started to jump over that side of his ship.

Geoffrey reached the captain in time to pull him back onto the deck.

"Below, Cyril!" he yelled. "Get the others!"

Geoffrey held Letchworth against him.

"We must do something, sir! My brother. . .going to be too late. . .if we do not act now. Henry is—"

"It is too late, Captain," Geoffrey said as gently as he could. "He is gone! Henry is gone! Look for yourself!"

Letchworth tried to avoid any sign of weakness since all crew members were now on deck, tried very hard to maintain that distance from them, however caring he might be, believing that some separation helped to reinforce his authority figure image as their captain, the man whose orders had to be obeyed, according to a long-standing maritime code that was in effect from one culture to another.

But Letchworth failed as he started to collapse, with Geoffrey catching him before he hit the deck.

"I should not have allowed him to get into this dangerous business," he sobbed. "Henry. . .he could have lived a quiet and safe life on a farm near—"

Several of the crewmen walked toward him, hoping to say something that would comfort the man, while others drifted over to the railing to fight the storm, the velocity of which would knock them on their backs if it did not blow them overboard.

"Praise the Lord Jesus!" one of them cried out.

Another called to Letchworth, "Captain! Look now! To the glory of Jesus, look!"

Geoffrey and the captain fought the wind and the driving rain to reach the railing, the cold causing them to shiver as they went, both gasping at what they saw.

Henry had not been swept away. He was holding onto the top fin of the baby whale which had managed to stay afloat in the violent, storm-stirred sea, not a surprising feat for an adult but somehow awe inspiring for one so young.

"Father God above!" Letchworth cried.

Henry yelled, "Hurry! Please hurry! So cold. . .my hands are slipping. . .almost numb. Save me!"

Some of the ropes that had held the baby whale were now thrown over the side toward Henry. He grabbed for one and missed it, tried again and missed that one. The third time he caught one end and held on tight. Working together, Geoffrey and Letchworth pulled Henry off the whale's slippery back as swiftly as they dared and then through the water until he was at the side of the ship, while trying to avoid banging him against the wooden hull.

"My hands are slipping again!" he called to them in panic.

He lost his grip and sank beneath the sea.

"You can't be lost now!" Letchworth declared above the roar of the wind. "I won't allow it, not this night!"

Geoffrey tried to restrain Letchworth, but in addition to his size, the captain had superior strength and broke away, diving over the railing. Geoffrey was preparing to go after Letchworth and Henry until Cyril grabbed him and pulled him back.

"You would be lost, too!" Cyril yelled, veins bulging on his forehead. "For the love of God, you must know that!"

A crew member shouted desperately, "Captain's got Henry! Throw the rope! Throw the rope quick!"

Both men spun around and saw Letchworth somehow managing to hold onto his brother and stay afloat. They tossed the rope over the railing. Henry reached out and grabbed it so firmly this time that the fibers cut into his palms. Several crewmen ran to the spot, grabbing the remainder of the rope on deck, and joined with Geoffrey and Cyril in pulling up the captain and his brother, who both were hanging onto that one strand.

Suddenly, as Henry's strength ebbed and he had to loosen his grip, the flesh being scraped off his hands, his feet slammed against Letchworth's shoulders and the captain was knocked back into the sea.

"Help him!" Henry screamed. "Do something to help him!"

Abruptly the wind seemed to change direction and the captain was swept away from the ship, his terrified expression made even more pitiable as everyone saw his mouth opening and closing but no sound that they could hear coming from it, and then he was gone, waters that he had mastered for many years now claiming him.

But Henry made it over the edge and onto the deck, desperately cold, crying, muttering incoherently, holding his raw hands at his sides because they hurt so much. Even so, he had to be kept from diving overboard again, and then, completely exhausted, he fell back against the hard wood, his body contorting while sobs tore through it, his crewmates gathered around, nearly all glancing out over the stormy English Channel as they whispered silent farewells to the man every last bloke of them had learned to respect and love.

TO BE CONTINUED. . .